What Looks Like CRAZY

Charlotte Hughes

JOVE BOOKS, NEW YORK

THE BERKLEY PUBLISHING GROUP
Published by the Penguin Group
Penguin Group (USA) Inc.
375 Hudson Street, New York, New York 10014, USA

Penguin Group (Canada), 90 Eglinton Avenue East, Suite 700, Toronto, Ontario M4P 2Y3, Canada
(a division of Pearson Penguin Canada Inc.)
Penguin Books Ltd., 80 Strand, London WC2R 0RL, England
Penguin Group Ireland, 25 St. Stephen's Green, Dublin 2, Ireland (a division of Penguin Books Ltd.)
Penguin Group (Australia), 250 Camberwell Road, Camberwell, Victoria 3124, Australia
(a division of Pearson Australia Group Pty. Ltd.)
Penguin Books India Pvt. Ltd., 11 Community Centre, Panchsheel Park, New Delhi—110 017, India
Penguin Group (NZ), 67 Apollo Drive, Rosedale, North Shore 0632, New Zealand
(a division of Pearson New Zealand Ltd.)
Penguin Books (South Africa) (Pty.) Ltd., 24 Sturdee Avenue, Rosebank, Johannesburg 2196,
South Africa

Penguin Books Ltd., Registered Offices: 80 Strand, London WC2R 0RL, England

This is a work of fiction. Names, characters, places, and incidents either are the product of the author's
imagination or are used fictitiously, and any resemblance to actual persons, living or dead, business
establishments, events, or locales is entirely coincidental. The publisher does not have any control over
and does not assume any responsibility for auhor or third-party websites or their content.

WHAT LOOKS LIKE CRAZY

A Jove Book / published by arrangement with the author

PRINTING HISTORY
Jove mass-market edition / March 2008

Copyright © 2008 by Charlotte Hughes.
Excerpt from *Nutcase* copyright © 2008 by Charlotte Hughes.
Cover design by Rita Frangie.
Interior text design by Laura K. Corless.

ISBN: 978-0-515-14423-9

JOVE®
Jove Books are published by The Berkley Publishing Group,
a division of Penguin Group (USA) Inc.,
375 Hudson Street, New York, New York 10014.
JOVE is a registered trademark of Penguin Group (USA) Inc.
The "J" design is a trademark belonging to Penguin Group (USA) Inc.

PRINTED IN THE UNITED STATES OF AMERICA

10   9   8   7   6   5   4   3   2   1

With love to Al Zuckerman—
a gentleman,
a man of great integrity,
and my personal hero

acknowledgments

With sincere appreciation to . . .

Janet Evanovich for giving me the opportunity of a lifetime.

Jen Enderlin for making me a better writer.

Donna Schaefer and Brenda Rollins, friends and proofreaders extraordinaire.

Rebecca George, a fine author in her own right, for her unconditional support.

Christine Zika for welcoming me to the Berkley family with fifty roses! Yes, fifty!

Jackie Cantor and Leslie Gelbman for helping me make this book the best it could be. And to Rachel W. W. Granfield, for her fine copyediting, and Jessica McDonnell, production editor. You guys rock!

Dr. David Berndt, clinical psychologist, for his professional input.

chapter 1

•••••••••••••••••••••••••

As a clinical psychologist, I've spent most of my time trying to convince my clients they're not crazy. The truth is, everybody is a little bit crazy; it's just a matter of degree. Take me, for example: I'm not exactly the poster lady for mental wellness, and I'm the one *treating* these people. I find that scary.

Even scarier is the well-dressed thirtysomething guy threatening to jump from the rooftop of the ten-story North Atlanta building housing my office. He's a new patient, referred to me by a psychiatrist I once dated.

Dr. Thad Glazer and I met while I was working on my doctorate at Emory University. Thad was blond and good-looking, and had inherited his father's comfy practice and love for Italian suits. Our relationship

1

ended when I caught him and his receptionist naked in his hot tub.

Thad limited his practice to medication management and referred patients to local psychologists for talk therapy, because he hated listening to people's problems. He amused himself by sending me the difficult cases—payback for breaking up with him and later marrying another man. Even more amusing to Thad was the fact that my marriage had hit the skids six months ago.

So that's how I ended up with Kevin "Wannabe Jumper" Bosley. And I had promised myself this was going to be a good day. I'd even dressed in my new yellow, white, and blue daisy skirt, and a yellow camisole. Just seeing it in the store had lifted my spirits.

"Listen to me very carefully, Kevin," I said, taking a step toward him, while carefully maintaining a respectful distance in case he decided to take me with him. That, and the fact that I am terrified of being on rooftops of tall buildings. "You do *not* want to do this. Suicide is *never* the answer."

"Back off, Dr. Holly!" he shouted. "You come any closer, and I'm bailing."

Beside me, my best friend and receptionist, Mona Epps, was frantically trying to reach Thad on her cell phone. I had pled, bribed, and tried to bargain with Kevin, to no avail. Thad was my last hope. Despite being somewhat superficial and self-centered, Thad usually came through for me.

"You must really hate your mother," Mona said, tossing Kevin a dirty look as she punched numbers on the phone.

Kevin blinked. "I don't hate my mother. What makes you say that?"

"Who do you think they'll call to the morgue to identify your body, you idiot! It's *always* the mother."

"You have no right to call me an idiot," he told her. "You don't know what I've been through."

"Oh, puh-lease," Mona said.

I shushed Mona. She was not the most diplomatic person in the world. Plus, she was annoyed as hell that she had broken a heel on her new Pradas as we'd chased Kevin six floors up the stairwell in our attempt to keep him from jumping. Fortunately Mona'd had the foresight to grab her cell phone, which was a good thing in case we needed to call 911, but by then it would be too late.

"Listen to me, Kevin," I said, trying to keep my voice steady, so that it would appear I was in control of the situation, even though my knees felt like tapioca pudding. "You can jump and put an end to your troubles, but what about the people who love you? What about those you leave behind? They'll be devastated. They'll blame themselves."

Kevin gave me an odd look. Someone who is depressed enough to take his own life generally does not give much thought as to how it will affect others.

"Thad's on the line," Mona said, offering me the phone.

"Hold on, Kevin," I called, taking the phone from her. "I've got Dr. Glazer—"

"I'm not talking to that egotistical bastard," he said. "Besides, this is his fault."

"Thad, I have a situation here with Mr. Bosley, the patient you sent me," I said quickly. "I could really use your help."

On the other end, Thad made a *tsk*ing sound. "Now, Kate, you know the rules."

I blinked. "What?"

"The rules, the rules," he said.

My frayed nerves were close to snapping. When Thad and I had been an item, he'd always insisted that I tell him what I had on beneath my skirt. It was a game between lovers that Thad still liked to play, despite our split. "Stop kidding around, Thad," I said. "This is an emergency."

"You either play by the rules or we don't play at all." I heard a smile in his voice.

"You are so childish!" I hissed, knowing he would find my annoyance even more amusing. "I've got a man ready to throw himself off the roof of my office building, and you expect me to describe my underwear?" Silence on the other end of the line. If Thad had been present, I would have personally drop-kicked his ass off the top of the building.

I turned and whispered into the phone. "Okay, dammit, they're black bikinis, cut high on the thigh and edged with red lace. Satisfied?"

"Give me a moment," Thad said. "I want to envision you in them."

I gritted my teeth. It would never occur to Thad that I was lying. He was the last man on earth I'd tell I was wearing plain, white, and very boring panties. I mean, why waste my Victoria's Secrets when I wasn't presently having sex? "Are you done yet?" I said.

"Okay, what's the problem?" he asked smoothly.

"Hello? Did you not *hear* me? Kevin Bosley is threatening to jump off the roof of my building!"

Thad sighed. "Damn, Kate, I send you a patient, and he tries to kill himself on the very first visit?"

"This is *not* my fault! He's angry because the medication you put him on—" I paused and lowered my voice again. "It's interfering with his sex life. Now, you need to get your butt over here and talk him out of jumping."

"It's not his medication, sweetheart. He was having problems getting it up when he came to see me. I put him on a mild antidepressant with few side effects, but he needs to give it time to kick in." Thad paused. "Look, even if I didn't have a tennis date, it would take forever to get to your office with the traffic. You're going to have to deal with this on your own, Kate."

I looked at Kevin. His arms were crossed, and one foot was tapping impatiently. "Why me?" I asked. "Why didn't you send him to his medical doctor? How do you know it's not a physical problem?"

"It's not a physical thing. His wife left him for his

best friend because their sex life was zero. Then, to make matters worse, he was fired from his job. I think he might have issues that led to his poor performance in the sack."

"What kinds of issues?"

"Who knows? Could be guilt. You'd be surprised how many guys let that sort of thing get in the way."

Oh, great, I thought. Another guilt-ridden man who couldn't get an erection because he just *knew* God had seen him whacking off to dirty pictures when he was fifteen years old, or because God knew he'd had lewd thoughts about some nun who taught him eighth-grade English at parochial school. My job was to listen respectfully to each sin and say, "Nope, that's not bad enough. What else have you got?"

"Why didn't *you* talk to him about all this?" I whispered.

"Kate, you know how it is. Guys don't like telling other guys they can't get it up. I mean, if you were some guy with a limp weenie, would you want to discuss it with somebody like *me*?" He laughed. "I can't relate to that sort of thing. By the way, if he jumps, your insurance will skyrocket."

"That's not funny, Thad."

"Hey, don't be like that. How about I make it up to you over dinner tonight? You could come to my place for steaks."

I knew steaks at Thad's house meant getting naked in his hot tub as well. I pressed the ball of my hand to my forehead, where I could feel a headache coming on. "I'm married," I said.

"Not for long," he reminded me. "It could be a pre-divorce celebration."

Thad didn't get it. My upcoming divorce did not inspire thoughts of cocktails and party favors. It hurt like hell to think about, so I kept shoving it aside in my head, sort of like moving an old chair into a corner because it didn't fit in the room. I didn't want to think about the divorce, and I especially did not want to discuss it with the man on the other end of the line.

"Good-bye, Thad." I hung up and regarded Kevin.

"Well? What did he say?" Kevin asked.

I stood there for a moment. "Dr. Glazer wanted me to tell you that you have every reason to be optimistic, because he used to have your problem and I was able to cure him."

An hour later I was lying on the sofa in my office, doing deep-breathing exercises. I'd convinced Kevin Bosley not to jump to his death, and I'd somehow managed to hold myself together for our session. Now *I* was a wreck. Multiplication tables fired through my brain, taught to me by my late grandfather, who'd been a math teacher and my only normal relative.

There is a certain order to math that doesn't exist in life. The world can blow up, but two times two is always going to equal four. For some weird reason, I find that comforting. I like even numbers. I prefer to start my day with an even number of ink pens in the oversized "I Love Atlanta" coffee mug on my desk. Mona knows this. Which is why, if I have eight pens in my mug, she'll drop in an extra just to throw me off.

"How'd it go with Limpy?" Mona said, coming inside my office.

Mona and her mouth, I thought. No wonder she'd flunked out of Miss Millie's Charm School. "We'll be seeing a lot of him."

"Why am I not surprised?" Mona plopped into the chair next to me and propped her feet on the coffee table.

Her housekeeper had obviously delivered another pair of pumps, because the wounded Pradas had been replaced. Mona wore only expensive designer fashions, and always looked great. She accessorized the reception room with her clothes.

"He'll pitch a tent in the hallway," Mona said. "People will think we're selling Rolling Stones concert tickets." She blew out a sigh. "What is it about men and their penises? It's all they care about. I mean, what about world peace, the rising crime rate, and unemployment? What about global warming?"

"Face it, Mona. A man who can't get an erection does not care if some polar bear doesn't have a place to hang his hat." I couldn't believe those words had come out of my mouth. I knew Kevin was in a lot of pain, and I'm normally sympathetic, but I was having a crap day.

"Could we change the subject?" I said. I did not want to think about men's bodies, because then I'd have to think about my soon-to-be-ex-husband's body. They didn't get any sexier than Jay Rush: tall, dark, and broad-shouldered, with bone-melting blue eyes and a charm-your-panties-off smile. And I'd walked out on him. You could have knocked me over with a feather when he didn't come after me. Now all I was waiting for was a judge to make the split legal.

"Sorry," Mona said. "I know you aren't supposed to discuss your patients with me, but they tell me everything, anyway."

I had tried to discourage my patients from sharing their problems with Mona, who would then feel compelled to offer advice. Mona's answer to everything usually involved a trip to the mall.

Mona could afford to shop all she liked. She was rich. After flunking out of charm school and beauty college, she had met and married Mr. Moneybags, aka Henry Epps, a much older man who'd made a fortune inventing a fish lure that bass found irresistible. Mona liked to say she'd made her money the old-fashioned way: she'd married it.

However, unlike most gold diggers, Mona had fallen in love with Mr. Moneybags and was devastated when he had a heart attack, fell off his bass boat, and drowned. She and I had met shortly afterward, when she attended a grief group I had set up. We became friends, and I became a frequent visitor to her house in Buckhead, which is where a lot of Atlanta's wealthy lived. Mona's house had more square footage than most strip malls.

"You seem depressed," Mona said. "You look like you could use a Prozac drip." She turned and reached behind the chair for the teddy bear we'd named Bubba. Some of my young patients preferred talking to me through Bubba. The wear and tear on his fur was proof that he made the little ones feel safe and secure in my office.

"Bubba, Dr. Holly isn't feeling well today," Mona said. "Could you please help her?" She put the bear right up to my face.

I sighed and closed my eyes, but it did not deter Mona. She changed her voice and pretended to be Bubba.

"Oh no, we have to help Dr. Kate," the squeaky Bubba voice said. "Tell her she should get a manicure."

I smacked my forehead. "Now, why didn't I think of that? You just solved all my problems, Bubba-Bear."

Bubba went on. "Uh-oh, Dr. Kate is not playing nice today. She is being rude. She does not appreciate that her friend Mona could be out having a good time instead of answering Dr. Kate's phone and putting up with her nutso patients."

I gave a sigh. Mona was not only mouthy but as politically incorrect as they came. I had told her time and again not to refer to my patients as nutso, wacko, or screwball, and not to call the reception area the Asylum Holding Room. Mona always said it was done in fun and, besides, she'd had enough therapy in her life that she'd earned the right to tell it like it was.

What could I do? Mona answered my phone for free. I'd tried to return the favor by teaching her to use a computer, and Mona was now able to shop online.

"Okay, Bubba," I said, taking him from Mona. "Tell Mona that Dr. Kate is sorry for being grumpy. Tell her that Dr. Kate is just stressed-out because she doesn't like having patients who try to jump off buildings. And Dr. Kate does *not* enjoy talking about men's penises, because she hasn't had sex in a very long time."

"Excuse me?" A voice sounded from the doorway. I looked around Bubba and found a mousy woman with brown hair and clunky eyeglasses standing at the door. I was certain she'd heard every word.

"Who are you?" Mona blurted.

"Alice Smithers," she said. She pushed her glasses high on her nose and looked from Mona to Bubba to me. "I have a one o'clock appointment to see Dr. Holly. I'm early. Am I in the wrong office?"

I wanted to put Bubba over my face and smother myself. Instead I raised my hand. "I'm Dr. Holly."

I had almost recovered from my embarrassment by the time Mona buzzed me to say that Alice Smithers had filled out her preliminary paperwork. As I invited Alice inside my office, I noted that she looked anxious. I didn't know whether it was a simple case of new-patient jitters, or whether she was second-guessing her choice of therapists, or both.

She sat on the sofa and clasped her hands together so tightly that her knuckles turned white. I attached her information sheet to my clipboard and took the chair beside her. I smiled and made eye contact, which wasn't easy considering that she knew how long it had been since I'd been laid.

Alice's gaze darted about the room before landing on my coffee table, where I kept a short stack of magazines, a bowl of potpourri-scented seashells, and a box of tissues.

"I'm Kate," I said, offering my hand. "Is it okay if I call you Alice?" She gave a quick nod, unleashed her right hand from the left, and shook mine.

A lot of therapists spend the initial visit getting a patient's complete history, beginning from the moment they slipped from their mother's womb. I don't do that. I have a short attention span, and my eyes glaze over by the time they reach third grade.

I *do* like to know whether patients are taking psychiatric medication, though. There are certain drugs that are attention-grabbers, and if a patient is taking one of them, I can pretty much bet I'm dealing with a psychotic. I want to make sure those puppies are currently on their meds.

Fortunately Alice Smithers did not look psychotic. She looked scared.

"So, how can I help you today?" I asked, noting her

interest in my latest copy of *National Geographic*. I'd started subscribing to *National Geographic* and *Smithsonian* magazine because I was treating a couple of gifted children. Those kids keep you on your intellectual toes.

"I never received this issue," Alice said sadly, "and I'm almost sure I didn't receive the one before it. I can't imagine why I'm not getting my copies. I'm paid up for the year. I should probably call and complain." She sighed. "I wish people would do what they're supposed to."

"I'll be happy to lend you my copy," I said.

She shook her head. "I prefer not to borrow things from people. I worry that I'll forget to return them. I used to have a good memory. Now I have to make notes to remind myself." She looked embarrassed.

"I'm forgetful, too," I said, trying to put her at ease. "That's why I stopped my Honor Snacks service. I kept forgetting to pay for them."

"And you ate the snacks anyway?" She looked aghast. "Oh, I could never do that."

"I always settled up with the company at the end of the month," I said defensively. I decided I'd dropped another notch in Alice's opinion. Finally I glanced down at her file, and saw that she was twenty-eight years old, single, a bookkeeper for an office supply store. No medication was listed. "How can I help you, Alice?"

She hesitated. "I don't know where to start. I saw your advertisement in the Yellow Pages, and the words 'caring and compassionate,' and I knew you'd understand."

Mona had added those two words to my ad, thinking it would draw more patients. Alice was the first to mention it.

"It's about my job," she said. "The absolute worst thing in the world has happened." She covered her face with her hands. "I am so embarrassed."

"Everything you say here stays in here," I said. I realized I sounded like that advertisement on TV where potential visitors were assured what they did in Vegas stayed in Vegas. Which sort of made me want to go to Vegas and find out what was going on in the town.

Alice took a deep breath. "Last Friday, my boss said he was going to have to let me go because his wife had found discrepancies in the accounts, and money was missing."

I didn't bother to hide my surprise. I could not imagine how a woman like Alice, someone who would lose sleep over a few missing quarters for Honor Snacks, had ended up in such a situation. But, then, people surprised me all the time. "How did you respond?"

"I told his wife I'd never stolen anything in my life." Alice choked back a sob. "Which is the absolute truth," she added.

She took off her glasses and reached for a tissue. I noted right away that, beneath the glasses and the tears, there was a very pretty woman who was, either consciously or unconsciously, doing a good job of hiding it.

"I'm sorry you're upset, Alice," I said gently. "Why do you think his wife made those accusations?"

"She—her name is Ellen—wants me gone," Alice said. "I was hired to fill her position when she left to have a baby a year ago. Now she obviously wants her job back. She's been coming in the past few weeks to answer the phone, and she watches every move I make." Alice sniffed and mopped tears. "If she comes back to work, they won't have to pay me. I think they're having financial problems."

"Is money missing?" I asked.

Alice shrugged. "I'm very conscientious. But Ellen took the accounts and ledgers from me, so I have no way of going back and checking for possible errors. She took my office keys."

"So your boss—"

"His name is Allen. Allen and Ellen Fender of Fender Office Supply," she added.

"Does Allen think you took the money?"

"I don't know. He wouldn't even look at me when he fired me. I think he's ashamed because his wife bullies him. Also, I think he's afraid I'll tell Ellen about his affair."

This was getting interesting. "Oh, so there's another woman in the mix?"

"I accidentally saw them together in Allen's office."

"Did you tell Ellen?"

"It's not my place."

"Did the Fenders threaten to press charges against you when they accused you of taking money?"

"Ellen said she wouldn't call the police if I left quietly. I told her I needed time to find another job."

I could see the anguish in her eyes. "Do you really think you can continue to work there after what you've been accused of?" I asked. "You must be furious." But Alice didn't appear furious. She looked like a whipped puppy.

"I don't get angry."

"Yes, but if you didn't take the money—"

"Of course I didn't take it!"

"Then you've been wrongly accused," I said. "You probably need to talk to an attorney."

"I can't afford to hire an attorney, and I don't think they can either. I suppose I should update my resume and send it out as quickly as I can. I can't believe they're treating me like this," she said. "I should have my head examined." Alice suddenly laughed. The laugh became a giggle. "I *am* having my head examined, aren't I?" she asked.

As surprised as I was to see the laughter, I joined in. People have no idea how genuinely healthy it is to laugh. I could see the tense lines softening in Alice's face. "Do you have trouble expressing anger?" I asked.

The smile faded. "I don't like confrontation. I hate confrontation. I'd rather be boiled in oil. I'd rather have bamboo shoved up my fingernails. I'd rather—"

"I think I get it," I said. "Most people don't like confrontation, but that doesn't mean you have to roll over and play dead. What the Fenders are doing to you seems very unfair." My own job suddenly felt less crappy.

Alice stared at me for a full minute, then put on her glasses and straightened her back. "You're absolutely right," she said. "I'm not going to make it easy for them. I'm going to tell them I do not appreciate being wrongly accused, and they're going to have to give me two weeks' notice. Plus I expect a good job reference. If they don't agree to that, then I'm going to threaten legal action."

The change in her was remarkable. Dared I hope that the woman had a streak of spunk in her? "Good for you, Alice!"

"Thank you for helping me, Dr. Holly."

"You're very welcome. And call me Kate."

Alice reached for her purse and stood up. She started for the door. "You haven't used all your session," I said.

"I'm done," she announced. She opened the door and walked from the room, pausing long enough to write a check and hand it to Mona.

Mona and I both watched her leave. "Damn," Mona said. "Is it me, or should we call the fashion police and have that woman thrown behind bars?"

"Not everybody can be as beautiful as we are," I said.

Mona picked up the appointment book. "When is she supposed to come back?"

"She's not," I said. "I seem to have cured her in one session."

Mona pressed her lips together and shook her head. "Not even Dr. Phil can cure patients in one session. He always tells the people on his show to get follow-up counseling."

Mona was a huge Dr. Phil fan and thought I should have my own show called *Dr. Kate*. "I guess I got lucky, huh?" I said.

"You can't build a successful practice like that, Kate. You need to spend more time with your patients. Milk it, you know?"

I didn't get a chance to respond. George Moss, another of Thad's rejects, threw open the door just then and stormed in. His bald head was slick with perspiration. The hair that remained stood in white tufts.

"You screwed up, lady," he said, pointing at me. "I came here asking for help. But you failed, and now my wife has left me." He pulled a vial from his pocket and shoved it in my face. "You see this? Do you know what this is?"

Mona and I exchanged looks. "A urine sample?" I said.

"Wrong. It's nitroglycerin. You make one false move, and you and your receptionist can kiss your sweet asses good-bye."

chapter 2

∙∙∙∙∙∙∙∙∙∙∙∙∙∙∙∙∙∙∙∙∙∙∙∙

I stood quietly and listened to George Moss rant and rave and threaten to blow Mona and me to smithereens with his vial of insulin. As an advanced diabetic, George was forced to monitor himself several times a day and carry his insulin and syringe with him.

Thad had been kind enough to warn me beforehand about Mr. Moss's hysterics, and I'd agreed to see the man anyway. But Thad had not warned me that George, a man well into his seventies, insisted on wearing his shirt partially unbuttoned so the world could see his gold chains and medallion. The world was also forced to endure George's bony chest, dotted with age spots and sprigs of gray and white hair. Bad enough that I had to deal with a histrionic, but I was always tempted to raise George's rate every time I caught sight of that bare chest.

"Mr. Moss?" I said, trying to make myself heard above his tirade. "You are going to have to calm down."

"Calm down?" he shouted. "Did you say calm down? After you've wrecked my life?" he demanded.

I knew George was perfectly capable of wrecking his life without my help. The man lived in constant crisis; like Mary's little lamb, drama followed George wherever he went.

"You are the worst therapist I've ever had," George said.

I nodded in agreement, even though I was almost certain there were worse therapists than me. Then again, maybe George was right. Maybe I should have been a math teacher like my grandfather. If a math teacher had a bad day, he could simply erase his blackboard, grab his grade book, and go home. A bad day for me could have serious consequences.

"Mr. Moss, please lower your voice," I said calmly. "I know you're upset, but I told you last time that I would not agree to hold a session with you if you threatened to blow up my office."

I looked at Mona, who was filing a fingernail. "Mona, Mr. Moss isn't feeling well today," I said. "Would you please reschedule him for next week?"

She nodded and began flipping through pages of the appointment book. "How about next Tuesday at three o'clock, Mr. Moss?" she said.

George's jaw dropped open in surprise. "You're kicking me out?" he said, taking a step closer to me. "You can't do that! This is an emergency!"

"Oops, three won't work," Mona said. "How about ten a.m.?"

George Moss looked from me to Mona and back at me. "I'll have your license for this. I'll call the American Psychological Association and report you."

"Take it or leave it, George," I said.

He exhaled, and all the air seemed to leave him. He nodded.

My house and office were both located in Perimeter Dunwoody, an area northeast of metro Atlanta. It hadn't been easy finding an affordable rental close to work. I hadn't taken that into consideration when I'd thrown my suitcases into my Toyota Camry and squealed from the parking lot of the loft I'd shared with Jay. I'd ended up at Mona's, where I spent three weeks drinking wine, crying on her shoulder, and watching Popeye cartoons on DVD. Mr. Moneybags had not only left Mona his mansion, his limo, and a gazillion dollars, but he'd also willed her his entire Popeye cartoon collection. Despite my Ph.D. in clinical psychology, I had yet to figure out why Popeye and Brutus were constantly coming to fisticuffs over a woman like Olive Oyl.

Unlike Mona's mall-sized home, my rental house was old and small. The front stoop sagged like a tired washwoman. The heating and air were unpredictable, as was the water heater, which meant that on a good day my hot shower lasted almost five minutes. Then, when I least expected it, the shower would run hot for fifteen minutes. Fuses blew, the ceiling leaked, and the refrigerator was on its last leg. Nothing was for certain; the house seemed to have mood swings. I'd named it "Mad Ethel." I didn't complain to my landlord for fear he'd actually make repairs and raise the rent.

As I climbed from my car, I noticed my neighbor across the street peering out her window. Bitsy Stout was a member of the Pilgrim's Praise and Abundance Church, located a few miles from our neighborhood in what used to be a China Buffet. Her minister obviously preached hell and brimstone. Bitsy felt her job was to scare small children into going to Sunday school, by telling them what God did to Sodom and Gomorrah and that they'd better clean up their act or else. That way, Bitsy didn't have to deal with trick-or-treaters or Christmas carolers coming to her house. Kids rode their bicycles two miles out of the way to keep from passing her home and getting a lesson on Hellfire 101.

I'd never believed in a wrathful God. There was enough scary stuff going on in the world, with my family, and in the office.

I stepped inside my front door. My mother and my aunt had decorated my house. They were junk dealers who scoured garage sales, landfills, and flea markets for their finds. My earliest memory was of them grasping my hands and lowering me into a Dumpster for a broken table lamp. They repaired and painted the items in fiesta colors, added stripes and polka dots, and sold them out of their driveway. Which was why my house looked like a flea market had thrown up in the living room.

The kitchen was at the back of the house. Its wooden cabinets were a dull brown, the wallpaper a 1970s pattern of ivy and latticework. The window looked out over a shaded, fenced-in yard in which the previous tenants had left a picnic table and where I sometimes drank my morning coffee and read the newspaper.

I looked inside my refrigerator. It held the bare necessities: a twelve-pack of diet soda, a pound of coffee, a bottle of soy sauce, and a single can of beer. My meals consisted of frozen dinners, canned soup, and takeout. I checked the freezer and saw that I was down to my last Salisbury steak dinner, which was about as appetizing as wood chips. I decided to wait. Later, when I got really hungry, it would sound more appealing.

I went upstairs to change. The only good thing that had come from my separation was all the weight I'd lost. In five and a half months, I'd dropped from a size ten to a size six. Before that time I'd dieted like every other red-blooded American woman. The bad news about losing weight was that, despite my having my clothes altered, they still hung on me. I could not afford a whole new wardrobe, but from time to time I got lucky and found something on a clearance rack. Had I been a size three, Mona would gladly have given me her seconds, and I would be wearing Gucci, Donna Karan, and Versace.

I slipped off my skirt and pulled on a pair of shorts. The elastic waist kept them from falling off. I caught my reflection in the mirror. Weekends at Mona's pool had bronzed and toned me, but my drab, dark brown hair needed something. Mona had a long list of suggestions for it, but I couldn't imagine sitting in a salon that long. I put it in a ponytail so I wouldn't have to think about it.

I'd barely made it downstairs when I heard the rumble of a truck. I knew that sound. My mother and my aunt had purchased a bright red 2007 Navistar CXT monster pickup truck to haul their junk. It weighed six tons and was twenty-one feet long. You could haul a lot of stuff in a truck like that—a small town, if you wanted.

The doorbell rang. I peered through the peephole and found my platinum-haired mother and my aunt standing on the other side of the door. They were identical twins, Dixie and Trixie, who still dressed alike, even in their midfifties. They wore their signature red overalls, the words "Junk Sisters" embroidered over their left breasts. They were exhausting. They were reminders that my family tree had shaky branches, that my gene pool was probably unfit for swimming. I considered slipping out the back door.

My mother raised a red and white bucket of fried chicken up to the peephole. "Open the door, Kate," she said. "We know you're in there."

My taste buds did a happy dance at the thought of fried chicken. But was it worth the high cost of dealing with two women who thought they looked good wearing turquoise eye shadow and two-inch fake lashes? You could sweep an entire house with those lashes. As if acting on cue, my stomach grumbled and growled.

I opened the door.

"We heard you had a bad day," my mother said as she and Aunt Trixie stepped inside, plucking their sunglasses from their eyes and looking me over carefully, as though checking for injuries.

"Mona called you?" I asked.

"Now, don't get mad," Aunt Trixie said. "She was concerned about you and felt bad that she'd already made plans for the evening."

Mona's plans included a twenty-four-year-old medical student. They'd met at a party. They'd been standing across the room from each other when their gazes met and locked. It was love at first sight, Mona claimed.

"I only have one piece of advice," my mother said.

I knew my mother had more advice than I would ever need. "What is it?"

"You can't save the world."

"She's right, honey," Aunt Trixie said.

I nodded and followed them to the kitchen. My mother was already looking through the cabinets. "Where are your dishes?"

"I haven't gotten around to buying any. I mostly use paper plates." I pointed to another cabinet.

"Trixie and I could have gotten you a good deal on dishes if we'd known," she said.

Aunt Trixie nodded. "We could have picked them up for next to nothing at an estate sale yesterday."

I shrugged. "I don't do much cooking."

"That's why you're so thin," my mother said. "I hope you're not getting one of those eating disorders." She shook her head sadly. "Mona said you'd let yourself go."

"Mona said that?" I asked, feeling a bit hurt.

"She didn't mean it in a bad way," Trixie said quickly. "She's worried that you're under too much stress. She says you almost never get manicures anymore."

"You don't have any flatware either?" my mother asked, opening and closing drawers until she came to one that contained plastic knives and forks and hundreds of tiny salt and pepper packets. "I'll bet you don't even have pots and pans. Trixie, make a list."

My aunt pulled a pad of paper from her purse and started writing. "It's no big deal, Mom," I said.

Aunt Trixie waved off my remark. "Let us take care of it," she said. "We're professionals."

I'd learned long ago not to argue with my mother and aunt, because they would do exactly what they wanted. Before long I'd have more cookware than most restaurants. I grabbed three diet sodas from the refrigerator and carried them to the table. "Thanks for getting the chicken," I said once we'd sat down and filled our plates.

Aunt Trixie patted my hand and winked. Unlike my mother, who worried and nagged me about every little thing, Aunt Trixie was the peacemaker, the one who wanted to make everything okay.

"I wish you'd been a teacher like your grandfather," my mother said. "It can't be good for you, working around all those crazy people."

I looked at her. This, coming from a woman who'd once delivered my forgotten sack lunch to school wearing oversized Bugs Bunny bedroom slippers and pink foam hair curlers. She had almost caused me to drop out in second grade. "They're not crazy, Mom," I said. "They have problems, just like anybody else."

"Well, I don't think it's healthy, listening to people's troubles all day. I would get depressed. In fact, you do look a little depressed. What do you think, Trixie?"

My aunt put her hand to my forehead as though checking to see whether I had a fever.

"Would you two cut it out?" I said. "I'm not depressed, okay?" I decided it was time to change the subject. "How is the move coming along?"

My mother smiled proudly. "Great. You should see the new showroom. The wood floors are beautiful. Tell her, Trixie."

"They're beautiful."

"I can't wait to see it," I said. My mother and aunt had become celebrity junk dealers after a reporter from the *Atlanta Journal-Constitution* interviewed them. That had led to an article in *Southern Living* and a segment on

Home & Garden Television. Suddenly people were coming from all over to buy their junk.

They'd learned to weld, and that had resulted in a bunch of whatchamacallits and thingamajigs finding homes in wall art and sculptures. High-priced decorators began calling for accent pieces, and the Junk Sisters, as my mother and aunt were referred to, designed tags and renamed the items "Junque."

They were forced to hire employees in order to meet demand, but they quickly ran out of garage space. Finally they purchased a building in an area known as Little Five Points, a bohemian-style neighborhood likened to New York's Greenwich Village and New Orleans' French Quarter, and they'd been hauling Junque over there for weeks in preparation for their grand opening.

"Have many people responded to the invitations?" I asked. Mona and I had spent a full day helping them write out hundreds of invitations to the event.

"We're going to have quite a crowd, even for a Sunday night," my mother said.

"Great." The grand opening was to be held on Sunday night to accommodate my cousin's band, who'd offered to play at a cut rate since they seldom had gigs that night. They called themselves the Dead Musicians, a group of five men with shaved heads, tattoos, and nose rings.

After a few minutes, I noticed a silence in the room:

my mother and aunt had stopped talking. While that normally would have brought me much relief, I had the feeling something was wrong. "What is it?" I asked.

My mother took a deep breath. "It's about the invitations."

"First, you have to promise not to get mad," Aunt Trixie said.

I knew the news wasn't good. "What?"

My mother looked at Trixie. "You tell her."

"No, *you* tell her."

"We invited Jay," my mother said.

I looked from one to the other to see whether they were kidding. The pucker between my mother's brows assured me it was no joke. "Why would you do that?"

"It wasn't intentional," my mother said. "Tell her, Trixie."

"It wasn't intentional, hon," Aunt Trixie said. "Jay was in the same checkout line at the Wal-Mart store. We got to talking—"

"He said a friend of his read about us and was interested in seeing some of our art," my mother interrupted, "so I pulled an invitation from my purse and gave it to him, and—"

"To give his friend," Trixie cut in.

My mother nodded. "And then I realized how rude it would look if I didn't give Jay an invitation as well."

"Our divorce is final in a little over two weeks, Mom. He would have understood."

"Honey, he looks just as good as he did before you split up," Trixie said.

Just what I wanted to hear, I thought. "Well, don't be hurt if he doesn't come," I said. "I'm sure he would be as uncomfortable as I would, under the circumstances."

"Oh, he's coming," Aunt Trixie said. "He told us he wouldn't miss it for anything. He even asked about you. Wanted to know how you were."

"Naturally, he was concerned about your weight loss," my mother said.

I looked at her. "You told him I'd lost weight? Mom, he's going to think I'm pining for him." For once, just once, I wished my mother and aunt would stay out of my business.

"Don't worry," she said. "I told him it was due to financial stress and the crappy place where you were living."

I buried my face in my hands. "Oh, gur-reat! He's going to think I can't manage my life now."

"What do you care what he thinks?" my mother said. "You're divorcing him."

I looked at her. "It's a matter of pride, okay?" I carried my plate to the trash. "I can't possibly go to the grand opening now," I said dully.

"Oh, honey, you have to come!" she said.

I shook my head. Just talking about Jay Rush upset me. Why would I want to see him and reopen all the wounds? "I can't, Mom."

"That's silly," she said. "He's going to think you're

afraid to see him." She shook her head. "This whole thing is silly. The two of you need to kiss and make up before it's too late."

I sighed. "It's already too late."

"Maybe not," she said. "I think he'd take you back if you asked."

"Hello?" I waved my hands in the air. "I'm not going back to him. Not after what I went through."

My mom folded her arms on the table. "That's not fair, Kate."

"He lied to me, Mom!"

"He tried to make you less afraid."

"He told me his job as a captain was less dangerous than a regular firefighter's. He said better technology and advances in fire science, blah, blah, blah, made fire-fighting much safer."

"Well, that's essentially true," she said, "but that doesn't mean the work is risk free."

"He could have *died*!" I reminded her. "It doesn't matter how many advances have been made. Accidents happen. Walls and floors cave in and trap people."

Which was exactly what had happened to Jay and a couple of men in his crew. They'd come very close to being killed. "Call me dumb, but I'm tired of offering up the people I love to the great Fire God."

She and my aunt were quiet for a moment. "Well, I'm not a bit sorry I married your father," she said after a moment.

I just looked at her. "I'm not sorry you married him

either, Mom, but it would be nice to have him around. You know?"

Aunt Trixie covered one of my hands with hers.

My mother folded her arms on the table and leaned closer. "You practically lived at that firehouse the last year your father was alive. You ate there, and you would have slept there if I hadn't forced you to come home and do your schoolwork."

Trixie patted my hand. "You were a daddy's girl, that's for sure. Why, I don't remember a parade when you weren't riding next to him in a fire truck. The man seldom left this house without you straddling his shoulders."

"You're interrupting me, Trixie," my mother said. "The point I'm trying to make is that Kate knew, even when she was nine and ten years old, how the department worked, and she attended more than one fireman's funeral. She practically grew up with Jay, and it was his dream to go to college and study fire science and become a great fireman like his daddy and—" She stopped. "And your daddy," she added, looking directly at me.

"What are you trying to say, Mom?" But I already suspected.

"You knew exactly what you were getting into when you agreed to marry Jay."

That's the thing about my mother. She doesn't beat around the bush, and she's about as diplomatic as Mona. Meaning she always tells me the truth, whether I want to hear it or not.

Finally I shrugged. "So blame me, but I have no desire to white-knuckle it every time Jay races to a burning
building. And I have no intention of becoming a widow
before my time or raising a child without a father. Like
you had to do," I added.

"You had Uncle Bump," she said.

"Right. How could I forget?" Uncle Bump's real name
was Harry, and he used to drink. A lot. One night he got
loaded and mouthed off to a biker named Fist. By the
time the cops showed up, Uncle Harry had three cracked
ribs, a couple of missing teeth, and a badly broken nose.
The doctor could never get the nose to set straight, so
Uncle Harry was forced to live with a small knot along
the bridge, earning him the nickname "Bump."

You'd think Uncle Bump would have given up the
booze after that, but I was forced to endure his bone-
crunching bear hugs and Wild Turkey breath until I was
twelve years old.

Then he met and married my aunt Lou. She chain-
smoked nonfiltered cigarettes and carried an ice pick in
her purse. My mother credited Aunt Lou with putting
Uncle Bump on the straight and narrow. She and Uncle
Bump quickly produced a son named Lucien. Aunt Lou
bought Lucien a BB gun when he was seven years old,
and he became known as Lucifer to the neighbors.

I did *not* want Lucifer to be the father figure in *my*
children's lives.

"I just have one piece of advice," my mother said.
"No marriage is without its share of problems."

"I know that." But Jay's and my marriage had been pretty close to perfect. There'd been so much sex going on, we'd added Antonio's Pizza Parlor to our speed dial, because nobody had time to cook. It took more than great sex to make a marriage, though. After a day of listening to everybody's problems, I need some kind of order. And security. I'd had little of either growing up.

Which was what I told Jay after his twenty-four-hour stint at the hospital where he'd been treated for a dislocated shoulder and a host of smaller injuries. I wanted him to take Uncle Bump's offer to come in as a full partner in his security company.

Jay stood his ground, even as I tossed my suitcases into the trunk of my car and slid behind the steering wheel that day.

My mother and aunt quietly cleared the table and put the bucket of chicken in the refrigerator. When I looked up, they were smiling. Something told me they weren't finished adding confusion to my life.

"We brought you a surprise," my mother said, and motioned me to follow them outside to their truck.

"It's not more furniture, is it?" I asked. "I don't have room in my house for anything else."

"You'll see," my mother sang out.

They opened the tailgate and pulled out something that had been wrapped in old moving blankets. At the very back of the truck were a dozen pots of rust- and burgundy-colored mums. "Give me a hand," my mother said as Trixie grabbed a shovel.

"What is it?"

"It's for your flower bed," she said. "Help me stand it up."

I held the top section as she unwrapped it, and Aunt Trixie began digging. It was a sculpture formed out of tin and wire and various other materials. I cocked my head from one side to the other. "What's it supposed to be?"

"Step back and look at it," my mother said.

I did as she said. I circled it several times, checking from all angles. "I guess I'm not much of an art expert."

Aunt Trixie hurried to the back of the truck and pulled out a small a bag of concrete mix. "We call it *First Man and Woman*."

It suddenly became crystal clear to me: a man and a woman formed together, vines encircling them. I looked more closely at the man—specifically, at his groin. "Is that what I think it is?"

"You're supposed to draw your own conclusion," my mother said, "but I'll give you one hint. It's not a fig leaf."

I turned to find my aunt dumping dry concrete mix into a hole in my flower bed. She reached for the hose. "Wait!" I said. "You're going to put it in my front yard?"

"Dixie, I told you she'd be surprised," my aunt said, squirting water on the concrete and mixing it with a stick.

35

"Honey, I wish you could see the look on your face," my mother said. "I wish we had brought the camera. Consider it a late housewarming gift," she said.

"But you've already done so much. I don't feel right accepting this. Really," I added.

The telephone rang inside. "I should get that," I said, hoping it was Mona. "Don't do anything till I get back."

I hurried inside and answered the phone. Sure enough, it was Mona calling from the ladies' room at the restaurant to see whether I was feeling better. "We have to talk," I said. "What time will you be home?"

"I might not go home tonight," Mona whispered.

"Oh."

"I know what you're thinking. You're thinking he's too young. Well, he's almost twenty-five."

"Why are you being so defensive?"

"Because I don't like it that people think it's okay for a man to go out with a younger woman, but it's not okay for an older woman to go out with a younger man."

"I didn't say that."

"You're thinking I'll look foolish, is that it?" She sighed. "Oh, crap, I probably shouldn't go home with him. I'm thirty-four. I can't possibly take my clothes off in front of a twenty-four-year-old man."

I could not imagine someone like Mona being self-conscious. She was blond, petite, and perfect. "Maybe you shouldn't rush into anything."

"I really like this guy, Kate. Actually, I'm pretty sure I'm in love with him. Now that I think about it, I care about him way too much to sleep with him on the first date."

I gave a mental eye roll. To Mona it probably made perfect sense.

"Plus, he hasn't come on to me. Uh-oh."

I could barely keep up with her train of thought. "What?"

"What if he isn't attracted to me? Oh, God, what if he's only going out with me because I'm rich?"

"Mona, you're talking in circles. You definitely need to slow down and reconsider."

"You're right, Kate. I lost my head for a minute. Lust does that to a person." She sighed. "So, what did you want to talk to me about?"

"Why don't we talk at the office tomorrow?" I suggested, knowing I needed to get outside and see what my mother and aunt were up to.

Aunt Trixie was holding the sculpture in place in the concrete, and my mother was planting mums. "You know, I was thinking that sculpture would look great in the backyard," I said.

"We're working on something for your backyard," my mother said, "but we won't be finished until Christmas."

I could only wonder with apprehension and dread what it would be. "Let me dig for a while," I said, noting that there were still a number of mums left to plant. At least it would take my mind off the sculpture itself.

An hour later we stepped back to admire my new

flower bed and sculpture. "I think it adds a nice touch to your entrance," my mother said.

"She'll be the envy of her block," Aunt Trixie said. "All your neighbors will want a sculpture like this." She tested the concrete with the toe of her shoe. "They'll have to get their own, though, 'cause this sucker isn't going anywhere."

chapter 3

....

The next morning, I opened my front door and found Bitsy Stout studying my new sculpture, a perplexed frown on her face. Her gray hair was tightly wrapped around pink foam curlers.

"What is *that*?" She pointed.

"It is garden art," I said.

I gave her my best smile. I prefer staying on Bitsy's good side, not only because her sermons have been known to scare large men but also because she makes the best sour cream crumb cake this side of heaven. It's an old family recipe, so secretive that it's written in a code not even the CIA can crack. The only way I can hope to get a taste is to suck up to Bitsy.

"It's a naked man and woman," Bitsy announced.

I locked my door behind me. "You're right, Bitsy. It's Adam and Eve. You know, from the Bible?"

"You don't have to remind me about scripture, young lady. I read my Bible from cover to cover every year." She leaned closer to the male figure. "And what is that thing sticking out right there?"

"A leaf?" I suggested innocently.

"That's no leaf!"

"Are you sure? It looks like a leaf to me."

She rose to her full height, which was no more than five foot one or two inches. "You should be ashamed of yourself, Kate Holly, for displaying nudity in your front yard. Think of the children!"

I wanted to tell Bitsy that children avoided our street because of her, but I was not willing to risk the consequences of making the woman angry. "It's religious art, Bitsy. Think Michelangelo's *David*."

"Religious art, my foot!" she said. "This is just another form of the pornography that is corrupting our world. It has to go."

"It can't go. It's set in concrete." I made a production of checking my wristwatch. "Oh, boy, I'm running late! Can we discuss this later over sour cream crumb cake and coffee?" I hurried to my car, climbed in, and made a quick getaway.

I arrived at work and found Mona in the small kitchenette in my suite of offices. Her silk dress was the color of cocoa, with tiny polka dots. I tried to guess the name of the designer. My outfit was a Jaclyn Smith, right off the Kmart rack. Jaclyn Smith's fashions are touted as "trendy and affordable."

"Coffee is almost done," she said. "You want a cup?"

I nodded and sat at the table. While Mona poured, I told her of Jay's intent to attend the Junk Sisters' grand opening. "No way am I going," I said, shaking my head.

Mona carried the cups to the table. "You *have* to go," she said. "If you don't, he'll know it's because of him."

"Why would I put myself through that?" I asked.

"I'll give you several good reasons. Jay broke your heart. It's payback time. Time to give him one last look at what he's giving up," she added. "We'll rub his nose in it, bring him to his knees, and watch him weep. By the time we're done, he'll rue the day he ever laid eyes on you!"

I looked at her. "Wouldn't it be easier to just tie him to the rear bumper of my car and drag his body through the streets?"

"Not good enough," Mona said. She eyed me critically. "Boy, have we got our work cut out for us. You'll need a complete makeover. You'll need a new dress. You'll need a manicure."

I heard the door open in the reception room down the hall. I glanced at the clock on the wall.

"That's probably Screwy Lewey," Mona said. "He's got a nine o'clock appointment."

I was too distracted to remind Mona that it was rude to talk about patients that way. I swallowed the rest of my coffee and hurried down the hall, where I found Mr. Lewey pacing.

He was in his late fifties, owned an auto parts supply store, and suffered from claustrophobia. My therapeutic intervention had included talk therapy, relaxation, and desensitization. My goal was to get him on an elevator, but just thinking about it often sent him into a panic attack.

"Good morning, Mr. Lewey," I said, leading him into my office. I motioned toward the sofa, and he perched on the edge, poised to bolt.

"I'm a little anxious," he said.

I took the chair next to him. I noted his shallow breathing. "What's going on?"

"I wanted to take the elevator. I stood there for twenty minutes trying to work up the courage to get on, but I couldn't. I ran up the stairwell as fast as I could. By the time I got to the fourth floor, I could barely breathe, and I was dizzy, and my heart was pounding."

"Running up four flights of stairs would leave most people breathless and light-headed," I said.

He met my gaze. "Oh. So maybe I wasn't really on the verge of a panic attack?"

"Maybe it was just your body warning you to slow down." I saw him relax. "Have you been listening to the relaxation tape we made?"

"I missed a couple of days because we had company. My wife's brother visited. I don't want him to know about my, um—" He paused. "My problem."

I nodded sympathetically. People who suffered from

panic attacks and phobias felt a lot of shame. They went to extremes to hide their fear. I knew from experience, because after my dad died, I'd had my share of them. It had taken three years of therapy to get them under control by learning to focus on something else until they passed. In my case, it was multiplication tables.

"What might your brother-in-law think?" I asked.

"He'd think I was nuts. Bad enough my wife has to know."

"You're close to your brother-in-law, aren't you?"

Mr. Lewey nodded. "I've known Ben for some thirty years now."

"What if the tables were turned? What if Ben had your problem? Would you think he was nuts?"

"Oh, no. I'd want to help if I could."

"But you're depriving him of the right to be helpful and understanding to you."

Silence.

"Suppose you had taken the elevator," I said. "And suppose it was full of people, and you had a panic attack. What's the worst that could happen?"

"I could die."

"Okay, what's the second-worst thing that could happen?" I asked, wondering if I'd ever be able to convince him he wouldn't die.

"If I had a panic attack, I would humiliate myself."

"How could you reduce your stress to lessen the odds of having one?" I asked.

He just looked at me.

"We've discussed this many times, Mr. Lewey."

"You mean where I get on the elevator and *tell* everybody what a nutcase I am? I'd rather jump from the top of this building."

I thought *I'd* go into a panic attack just hearing those words. "I have a new rule that forbids patients from jumping off the roof," I said, "so you'll have to find a different way to handle your stress. What if you got on the elevator and stood at the front, where you could simply push a button and stop it on the next floor?"

"I might get dizzy and not be able to see the buttons."

"Perhaps you could ask the person next to you to push the button."

"They'd want an explanation."

"Not necessarily."

He sat there quietly, and I could almost see the gears turning in his mind. I could also see that he was becoming anxious just thinking about it. "What is your level of anxiety?" I asked him.

He swallowed. "About a seven," he managed.

"Okay, close your eyes and visualize a place you find calming." We worked for several minutes as Mr. Lewey focused on sitting on a deserted beach, watching a sunrise and smelling the briny air.

In his mind, through hypnosis and guided imagery, Mr. Lewey had ridden the elevator many times. We spent the remainder of his session practicing. He was noticeably relaxed by the time we finished.

"I really want to be able to get on that elevator," he said.

"You will," I promised.

I barely had time for another cup of coffee before Martha and Jack Hix arrived for couples therapy. As a therapist, I'm not supposed to take sides, but if I'd been Jack Hix, I would have hit the road a long time ago. Martha was a nag of the worst kind.

Spouses who live with nagging often learn to tune it out, which is what Jack Hix had been doing. That only made Martha's badgering louder and sometimes, as in the Hixes' case, verbally abusive.

Jack Hix had become adept at ignoring his wife. The guy had perfected visual imagery. When Martha walked into the room, Jack surrounded himself with a force field that would have blocked Darth Vader. It also blocked the sound of Martha's voice.

There are times in a person's life when he has to hear what the other person is saying, even if that person is a bona fide nag. Like in the event that your wife is stung by a bee and has an allergic reaction. Which is precisely what happened to Martha one day while she was pruning her rosebushes.

Jack's so-called force field had prevented him from noticing that Martha had swollen to twice her normal size and couldn't breathe. He'd been channel surfing in front of a blaring TV when the EMS crew showed up.

In a fit of rage, Martha had thrown a candy dish at him, and Jack had ended up with six stitches in his forehead.

Therapists refer to these people as high-risk couples because, if one of them loses it in a session, somebody can get hurt. You have to set ground rules with these couples from the start so that they'll respond when you call a time-out.

"How'd it go this week?" I asked.

"I did exactly what I was supposed to," Jack said. "When Martha spoke to me, I listened, and I repeated her words verbatim so that she would know I'd heard her."

I looked at Martha. "Did you feel validated?"

"Yes. I did what you said to do. I told Jack what I needed from him without nagging or belittling. We had to take a couple of time-outs when one conversation became heated. I went into my sewing room until I calmed down."

"Excellent!" I said. There'd been a time when I did not think the Hixes capable of saving their marriage, but I had seen a number of couples change their behaviors so that they could live in harmony. I liked to think I played an important part.

But, then, what the hell did I know? My own marriage had hit the skids after only a few short years.

Over lunch, Mona told me about her date with the twenty-four-year-old medical student, Liam. He was very mature for his age, she claimed.

"I've decided not to sleep with him," Mona said.

I felt my eyebrows arch high on my forehead. "Ever?"

"He has to prove his intentions so I don't have to worry that he's just out for my money."

"You've only had one date with him, for Pete's sake. Isn't it a little early for him to start slaying dragons?"

"Have you ever met a man, and you instantly *knew* he was *the one*?" she asked dreamily. "I'm talking once-in-a-lifetime, love-of-your-life kind of stuff."

I felt a giant fist squeeze my gut. I knew exactly the kind of love she was talking about. I'd fallen hard and fast for Jay Rush. It was the only reason I could think of that had made me ignore the warning bells when I agreed to go out with him.

I had finished graduate school and was working at a county mental health center when I walked into an ale-house one night with several coworkers and spotted Jay Rush. I had not seen him since my father's funeral, where I overheard one woman tell another how good-looking fifteen-year-old Jay Rush was turning out. He had bedroom eyes, she said. With those eyes, all he'd have to do was look at a girl to get her pregnant, the woman had added.

I'd been ten years old at the time. I made a point not to even look in Jay's direction.

I found it hard not to stare at him that night at Paddy's Alehouse. He was surrounded by firemen who were toasting his new promotion to captain. As though feeling my eyes on him, he turned, and our gazes connected. He put down his drink, rounded the bar, and gave a low whistle.

"Little Katie Holly," he said.

I shrugged. "I'm all grown-up now."

He'd studied me closely. "So, what are you doing tomorrow night?"

Now, even after six months of being alone, I had no desire to meet anyone. Deep down, I knew they'd all fall short. But I could not love a man as much as I loved Jay and live with the constant fear of losing him. I've learned that everyone has a fear of something. Mine was loss. Better to get a cat. Cats are almost indestructible, and they never notice when you get bloated once a month.

"Take your time with this guy, okay?" I told Mona after a moment. "It has only been a year since Mr. Moneybags died. I mean, Henry." I checked my wristwatch. I still had an hour to kill before my next patient. I could catch up on my paperwork. I could look through the professional journals piling up on my desk. I could take a nap.

"Oh, before I forget," Mona said. "Don't make plans for Saturday. Francois is going to meet us at the salon at ten a.m. for your makeover."

Francois was Mona's hairdresser and all-around beauty consultant. "I can't afford Francois!"

"It's not going to cost you anything. He owes me. Who do you think helped him get his start when his name was just plain old Frank and he didn't know a word of French?"

I went into my office, sat at my desk, and counted the pens in my coffee mug. Ten of them. That calmed me somewhat. It lasted until I reminded myself that I would see Jay in three days. I started doing multiplication tables in my head.

Our initial court appearance had been brief, and I had avoided looking at him. I'd felt, after four months and no word, that it was time to file for a no-fault divorce and get on with my life. Even then, he hadn't called. I'd known he was stubborn and proud—he spent half his life living in a dormitory setting with other macho firefighters—but I had expected more from him. I had expected him to offer some sort of compromise—*anything*. But it didn't happen. In my opinion, being a cop or a firefighter is sort of like being in the Mafia. Once people join up, they seldom leave.

So I moved into Mad Ethel.

There had been no property to settle; Jay had contributed solely to our savings, and he'd bought the upscale loft before we'd married. I'd used what little money I had to pay off student loans and start my practice. I'd asked for nothing, and I'd insisted on having my name removed from Jay's assets. My attorney had promised to appear on my behalf at the final hearing, because I had no desire to listen to a judge formally pronounce Jay and me divorced.

I did not want to see Jay. I did not want to look into

those intense blue eyes and be reminded of all the good times. I did not want to think about the great sex, about falling asleep in his arms and waking up to the sound of him setting a fresh cup of coffee on my night table. I had no desire to rub his nose in what he'd lost, because I'd lost out as well. Maybe it *was* my fault for letting those old fears creep into my life once more. I probably needed more therapy. So far I'd done a lousy job trying to analyze myself.

My private line rang, and I picked up. Thad was on the other end. "George Moss called me," he said. "He told me what a terrible therapist you are." Thad sounded amused.

"Yeah, well, George is a terrible patient," I said, "so I guess that makes us even." I told him how George had acted.

"You don't owe me an explanation, Kate. Let him find somebody else to abuse. Not that it's going to be easy for him. He's worn out his welcome with about half the therapists in this town."

"I'll see how he acts the next time he comes in," I said. I gave a sigh.

"You sound down. Bad day?"

"Mona thinks I need to go on Prozac."

"Are you exercising?"

"Not exactly."

"Isn't that what you'd recommend if a patient told you he or she was depressed?"

"Yeah."

"I could put in a pool. We could swim together."

I knew what Thad was capable of under water. "That's a little drastic," I told him. "I'll force myself to start walking on a regular basis," I promised.

"You need to let go of the past, Kate, and look to the future. I could play an important role in your future, you know."

"We already tried that," I reminded him.

"Yeah, but I was immature and self-centered at the time. I'm a whole new man. I'm what you'd call sensitive."

I almost laughed at the thought of Thad trying to pass himself off as Mr. Touchy Feely. "It's too soon for me," I said.

"Well, if you change your mind, you know where to find me. The only thing I ask is that you call first. You know, just in case I'm tied up? In case one of those religious people is at my front door. It's hard to get rid of them."

"I understand completely," I said.

I arrived home to find my sculpture draped in a bedsheet. I glanced across the street and saw Bitsy Stout peering at me through her window. I pulled the sheet off, went inside my house, and tossed Bitsy's sheet into the trash can.

I ate a piece of leftover chicken and took a walk. It was a start. Although it was still light outside, I could see families inside their houses, gathered at dining room tables. I passed a man in one yard, pitching a ball to his son.

I felt the familiar lump in my throat, and I was okay with it because it beat the hell out of sitting alone inside my house, which I had spent too many months doing. Granted, people had a right to grieve, but I was tired of grieving. I'd seen too many patients get comfortable in their grief; they wore it like an old sweater. Friends and family made excuses for them. Less was expected. I did not want to live like that.

Thad was right: I had to move on.

By the time I headed home, I'd made a decision. I was tired of feeling crummy about my ruined marriage and my life in general. I was ready to start living again. There was possibility and adventure and real joy out there, and I was ready to find it. It was not likely to knock on my front door, turn off my television, and drag me from the sofa.

I got so excited at the prospect of the new and adventuresome life that lay ahead that I started jogging. I hadn't jogged since college. I made it two blocks before I got a stitch in my side and became dizzy, but I ignored it. By the time I reached my front door, I was nauseous. Maybe I was overdoing it. Maybe I should ease slowly into my new life instead of jumping in with both feet and swimming toward it madly.

I unlocked my door, crossed the living room, and fell in a heap on my sofa. I reached for the remote control and turned to The Movie Channel because I could usually count on films to have happy endings.

On Friday, I saw one of my patients out and returned to my desk to work on my progress chart. I had made a list of short- and long-term goals. I was going to start taking better care of myself. I was going to stop eating frozen dinners and takeout, and I was going to start preparing healthy meals so that I didn't clog my arteries with gunk. Next to my list of goals was my grocery list, all fresh vegetables. I would need to buy a vegetable steamer. I added it to my list. Maybe I'd become a vegetarian or a vegan. I'd go to dinner with friends and they would applaud my disciplined lifestyle when I turned up my nose at red meat.

I tried to imagine a life without steaks or burgers. What would I eat fries with?

I asked myself whether I was using my lists and charts as avoidance behavior so that I didn't have to think about seeing Jay. I began making a list of what signs to look for in avoidance behavior.

"Kate?"

I looked up and found Mona standing in the doorway. I hoped I wasn't going to have to hear about Liam, because I'd already learned more about him than I wanted to know. "I'm sort of busy," I said.

Mona stepped inside and closed the door. "Alice Smithers is outside," she said quietly. "She asked if you could possibly work her in this afternoon. She doesn't look so good, and her outfit is all wrong."

I gave an inward sigh. I knew I had no choice but to see Alice. My next patient wasn't due in for half an hour.

That's the problem with being a psychologist. People are always expecting you to help them solve their problems, even when your own life has fallen into the toilet.

"Okay, send her in," I said. I gathered up my lists and charts and stuffed them into my center drawer. I stood and greeted Alice. Behind her, Mona was making faces and pointing to Alice's clunky shoes. Indeed, they wouldn't have been my first choice. "Please sit down, Alice," I said as Mona closed the door.

Alice sat on the sofa. "I'm so sorry to just barge in on you like this, Dr. Holly, but my situation is desperate."

I took the chair beside her. "What has happened since I last saw you?"

"I've made a grave error. I was so worried about finding another job and trying to pay my bills on time that I decided to get a roommate."

"That was quick," I said.

"Her name is Liz Jones. She's a cocktail waitress. Last night was her first night, and she invited her boyfriend over. His name is Roy. I could tell he was a big loser the minute I laid eyes on him. They drank and played music all night. I don't think I got more than ten minutes' sleep. Not only that, they trashed my kitchen and raided my refrigerator."

"Did you say anything to her?"

"Oh, no, I couldn't possibly."

"I see." Stupid me. I'd forgotten Alice preferred vats of boiling oil to confrontation.

"Besides, they were still in bed when I left."

"Did you ask Liz for references before you agreed to let her move in?"

Alice looked down at her feet. Her face was red, and I could tell she was embarrassed, but I didn't know whether it was due to her circumstances or whether she'd just realized what bad taste she had in footwear.

"No," she said. "I know it was a bad decision, Dr. Holly, but—"

"Kate," I said.

Alice nodded and yanked several tissues from the box. "My life is such a mess."

I nodded. If I had a dollar for each time I'd heard those words, I could afford to live next door to Mona. "How are things at work?"

Alice shrugged. "We've sort of called a truce while I look for another job. I sent out several resumes, but I haven't heard anything. It's too soon." She removed her glasses and mopped fresh tears. "Boy, I really screwed up."

"Sounds to me as though Liz, not to mention her boyfriend, is only adding more stress to your life, and that's the last thing you need," I said. "You may have to ask her to leave. And tell her to take Roy with her," I added.

Alice began wringing her hands. "I don't know. I was really counting on that money. She promised to have five hundred dollars for me on payday. That's half my mortgage payment."

"You didn't ask for money up front?" I asked, trying to keep the amazement out of my voice.

She gave an enormous sigh. "No."

I didn't know what to say. It was just unfathomable that Alice Smithers would take in a complete stranger without references or at least some kind of deposit.

"I know I did a stupid thing," she said. "I know I'm going to have to push for the money and set ground rules, even if it kills me."

"Most definitely," I said, hoping we had made some progress.

On Saturday morning Francois ushered us through the back door of his salon and led me to a chair. It was all very chic, with soothing spa colors. Francois wore black skintight denim with a loose-fitting white linen shirt. He picked through my hair and gave a dainty sniff. "Dees hair does not vork. Eeet is all vrong."

I looked at Mona. "What did he say?"

Mona shrugged. "I have no idea. Cut out the gay Frenchman act, Frank. Speak English."

"The hair sucks, babe," he said, sounding more like a bartender in a cowboy bar.

"Can you do anything with it?" Mona asked.

"It can be salvaged, but she'll need a good cut, and I strongly recommend a new color."

I looked from Mona to Frank. "You're going to dye my hair? I don't want you to dye my hair." Frank gave me a hard look, threw up his hands, and stalked away.

Mona frowned. "Great! You just hurt his feelings."

"I don't want him to dye my hair!" I repeated, knowing I sounded like a broken record. "I thought I was here to get a trim."

"The man is a professional," Mona said. "He knows his stuff."

"He might know hair," I whispered, "but he doesn't know squat about French. That's the worst French accent I've ever heard."

We both looked toward Frank. He was sitting at the far end of the salon, arms crossed, chin hitched high. "What's he doing?" I asked.

"Pouting." Mona hurried toward him. "Frank, Kate is so sorry she hurt your feelings. She is very confused and depressed right now, which is why she let herself go to begin with. Please forgive her."

He sighed. Finally he stood and walked toward me. "Here's the deal," he said. "Your hair is too long. It makes your face droop, and that adds age. I can cut it, add highlights, and take ten years off your face. It's your call."

I knew my mouth was hanging open. I had not realized I looked that awful. Bad enough that I was shaking in my heels at the thought of seeing Jay again; I didn't want him to think I'd turned into a hag. "You can really make me look ten years younger?"

"Give or take a couple of years. I'll have to call Collette in to do your makeup." He picked up my hand, studied my nails. "Oh, hell." He dropped my hand. "I'll have to call Paulette to do your nails."

He looked at Mona. "You are going to *so* owe me."

It was after five by the time I left the salon with Mona at my side, my makeover complete. I didn't recognize the woman who'd stared back at me in the mirror once Frank, aka Francois, and his team of experts had finished. All I could do was gape at the incredible job they'd done. My long dark hair had been streaked with reddish-gold highlights and cut in a sassy style that barely grazed my shoulders. My makeup was flawless, and I had been given careful instructions on how to reproduce the look on my own, which accounted for the large bag of beauty products I carried.

Mona and I climbed into her Jaguar and sat there for a moment. She grinned. I grinned. "I look really good, don't I?" I said, having witnessed Francois's weeping over me—the masterpiece he'd created with his own hands.

"You rock."

"Good. May we eat now?"

"Before or after we look for your dress?"

"Dress?"

"Honey, you have to get a dress. I recommend short, black, and sexy. You'll need high heels to go with it, too. And you'll need a thong."

"Why do I need a thong? I don't even like thongs."

"Not only are you going to *wear* a thong, you are going to find a way to let Jay *know* you're wearing a thong."

"Oh," I said. I wasn't sure how I was going to work it into the conversation, but Mona had steered me right so far.

Mona turned the key in the ignition, and her Jaguar purred. "Poor Jay," she said. "By the time we're finished with him, he's going to wish you'd just tied him to the back of your car and dragged his body through the streets."

chapter 4

....

I was dressed in my new size-six black dress and my new stilettos, waiting by the front window for Mona to arrive. Some people were meant to wear stilettos, but I am not one of them. I had been practicing walking in them for the past hour, but I was still an accident waiting in high heels.

I was also a nervous wreck, knowing that it wouldn't be long before I'd see Jay again. I'd never taken psychiatric drugs or tranquilizers, but I would have considered popping a Valium right about now. I probably could have asked Thad to write me a prescription, but that would have meant a trip to his hot tub, and God only knows what else. Better to risk a full-fledged nervous breakdown, I thought.

As Mona's white stretch limo pulled onto my street, I

reached for my small black evening bag, which held the bare necessities: house key, lipstick, cash, and a hair pick.

I hurried out, pausing briefly to lock my front door. As I walked toward the limo, I noted Bitsy's face pressed against her window, her mouth forming a giant O. It was hard to say what shocked her more: the limo or my dress, which left little to the imagination.

Mona's chauffeur, Jimbo, met me at the door of the limo and opened it for me. From Mona, I had learned the correct way to get into and out of a limo. I sat on the edge of the seat—facing outward—and very daintily swung my legs around before Jimbo closed the door. According to Mona, presentation is everything when getting into and out of a limo.

"Da-yum," Mona said. "I barely recognize you. I think you gave Jimbo a hard-on. If he drives into a tree, it's your fault."

My stomach growled in response. Mona arched one brow. "I haven't eaten all day," I said.

"You want a candy bar?" She reached for her purse.

"I can't eat. This dress is way too tight. There's not even room for me to eat a peanut. If I put anything in my mouth, my head will blow off."

"Hey, no exploding body parts in this vehicle," Mona said. "You save that crap for cabs. Cab drivers are used to that sort of thing. I once went out with a cab driver named Kahil. You wouldn't believe what goes on in the backseat of a cab."

"Pretty disgusting stuff, huh?" I said.

Mona shrugged. "That's the real world."

I just looked at her. What did Mona know about the real world? She'd lived like a princess for more than a decade. The shimmering dove gray dress she wore had probably cost twice my monthly rent. And what did she know about hunger? She could eat anything she liked and still be a size three. A normal-sized woman looked like a Wal-Mart Supercenter next to Mona.

"Guess what Liam and I did last night?" Mona said.

"You had sex?"

"No, we ate Ben & Jerry's ice cream and watched Popeye cartoons until two a.m."

I couldn't hide my disappointment. "I thought that was *our* special thing. I can't believe you did that with some guy you barely know."

She looked at me. "You're in a sour mood."

"Yeah, sorry," I said. "I should never have agreed to this."

"You look nervous. You look like you're on the verge of a breakdown."

"Of course I'm nervous," I said. "I haven't seen Jay in six months. And I'm annoyed at my mother for inviting him to the grand opening and putting me in this position." Plus my thong had slipped inside my butt crack, which I found pretty disgusting.

"Jay is going to want you back, sure as hell."

I gave an unladylike grunt. "We're talking about a man. He probably met somebody as I was squealing out of the parking lot." I had tried not to think along those lines because it hurt too much, but it was possible that he was already involved with someone. Not that he didn't have a right, I reminded myself.

"I'm glad Liam is different from other men," Mona said. "He's sensitive. Did I tell you he has dimples?"

"Yes, I believe you mentioned it a few thousand times."

Mona spent the rest of the drive discussing Liam, and it was up to me to either listen or bail out of a fast-moving car and risk death. We arrived at Little Five Points and found the neighborhood in full swing, despite its being Sunday night. No doubt the tourists hoped to catch the end-of-the-month and back-to-school sales.

Not only did tourists enjoy the area, but it also appealed to the artsy bunch, the Rasta knowledge-seekers, the tattooed, the pierced, the Goth, as well as the hip and young. It had deteriorated thirty years earlier due to racial unrest and a host of other problems. It became a haven for illegal activities, and violence had spread like a pox. But the people had fought back, and grants were approved to revitalize Little Five Points.

The limo stopped in front of my mother and aunt's building, where a sign read JUNQUE GALLERY AND FURNISHINGS. Mona was the first to step out. Her movie-star appearance drew stares. That she looked younger than I did, despite our being the same age, proved her Botox injections were working. I appeared right behind her, taking great care not to fall off my four-inch heels. The late August humidity was so thick, you could hang it on a clothesline. I noted the looks aimed my way, and offered up a prayer of thanks to Francois and company.

Uncle Bump met us just inside the front door. He looked me up and down. "Holy Moses, Kate, is that really you?"

Beside him, Aunt Lou took a long drag of her nonfiltered cigarette and looked equally impressed. "Work it, girl," she said. Her smoker's voice sounded as though it had been put through a paper shredder.

"Whoa, Kate!"

I winced inwardly at the sound of Lucien's voice. I glanced in his direction and wondered how I could be related to a man with so many tattoos and pierced body parts.

"You are *hot*!" he said, his eyes bulging and his shaved head shiny with perspiration. "Too bad you're my cousin, know what I mean?" He stuck out his tongue and wagged it in front of me. I shuddered at the sight of the stud through the very tip.

Aunt Lou stepped close to him. "You do that again, and I'm going to put my cigarette out on your tongue."

Lucien gulped and closed his mouth.

"Let's move on," Mona said breezily, taking my arm and steering me toward one of several portable bars.

The large showroom was filled with people wearing everything from tuxedoes to caftans and jeans. An enormous sculpture made up of an assortment of clocks sat in the very center of the room, surrounded by smaller sculptures. Furniture of every imaginable design and color hugged the walls. Mona and I sipped wine and looked about.

"I don't see him," I said, wondering how I could be immensely relieved and disappointed at the same time.

"He'll be here, don't worry," she insisted.

"Kate!"

I heard my mother's voice and turned. She and Aunt Trixie hurried toward us. They wore matching black satin overalls with corsages of white tea roses. They stopped short and stared.

"You look absolutely stunning," my mother said. "Doesn't she look stunning, Trixie?"

"Stunning," Trixie said. "And look at Mona."

"You look like celebrities," my mother said, "except that you're so thin."

"We have to stay thin and beautiful while we're still able to breed," Mona said.

She smiled at Mona. "By the way, thanks for telling all your rich friends about our little store. You wouldn't believe how many of them have come in."

"That's nice," Mona said and slipped me a smile.

I knew that smile. I also knew that Mona, the youngest widow in her neighborhood, had, in exchange for certain favors, vowed to discourage her friends' husbands from offering her a comforting shoulder after Mr. Moneybags died.

A waiter suddenly appeared. Tall flutes of champagne

filled his tray. Mona and I drained our wineglasses and exchanged them for the bubbly. We took turns toasting the Junk Sisters.

Aunt Lou hurried up and tapped my mother on the shoulder. "Some uppity-looking woman is asking about one of the sculptures. Y'all might want to talk to her." She made stabbing motions with her cigarette toward a woman who seemed to be admiring a piece.

"We'd better get over there," my mother said. She and Aunt Trixie promised to catch up with us later.

I had just finished my second glass of champagne and was feeling its effects when Jay stepped through the front door, his dark head several inches higher than most of the men's in the room. He was wearing a beige linen blazer, a blue shirt that matched his eyes, thigh-hugging blue jeans, and Doc Martens. The air left my lungs in one giant whoosh. Mona followed my gaze.

"Holy hell," she whispered. "There should be a law against a man looking that good."

My body turned hot and cold all at once. I felt light-headed. "We shouldn't have come."

"Maybe we can talk him into taking you back," Mona whispered.

I blinked several times. "What! That is *not* the plan."

"I'm thinking maybe we need a new plan."

"Oh, no, he's coming this way!" I turned and nudged her. "Stop staring!" I hissed. "Act like you don't see him."

"You're kidding, right?"

"Katie, is that you?"

His voice hadn't changed. It still made the tiny hairs prickle on the back of my neck. I looked up and pretended to be surprised to see him. "Jay, what are *you* doing here?"

"I was in the neighborhood," he said, his gaze fixed on me. "You look fabulous, Katie." He turned to Mona. "So do you. I saw your car out front. Does that thing come with a full bath?"

"I decided to put in a pool instead," she said.

He grinned. Mona and I smiled back. The three of us just stood there for a moment. "Hope I'm not interrupting anything," Jay finally said.

Mona jumped. "Uh, no, I was just leaving." She took off as though propelled from a circus cannon.

Jay chuckled and watched her go. "Was it something I said?"

I shook my head, but I couldn't think of a clever response. My spine had turned to jelly. Another waiter appeared with a tray of champagne. Jay traded my empty glass for a fresh one. "To the Junk Sisters," he said, touching his glass to mine.

I took a tentative sip. The last thing I needed was another drink. "So, how is life treating you these days?" I asked, falling back on the oldest cliché in the world so that I wouldn't just stand there salivating like Pavlov's dog. Obviously life had been treating him very well, because he had never looked better. I'd forgotten just how blue his eyes were, or maybe they just *appeared* bluer because the summer sun had bronzed his olive complexion and left a light sheen on his hair.

"I'm good," he said. "Looks like you're doing pretty well yourself." He gave me a thorough perusal. "Great hair, great dress, great body. If you looked any hotter, I'd have to call for a fire hose."

I met his gaze. "Thank you, Jay."

"You're welcome."

We stood there and smiled at each other. Smiled and nodded and looked about the room, and nodded some more. I didn't know what to say. What *do* you say to the love of your life once you've discovered the relationship isn't going to work out?

"I've missed you, Katie," he said.

It was absolutely the last thing I'd expected to come out of his mouth. My stomach began to flip-flop like a fish pulled from the water. At the same time, I was slightly annoyed. I drained my glass. "That would explain the cards, letters, and phone calls." The words leapt from my tongue before I could reach out and snatch them back.

Jay's grin, which would have made old ladies thankful for adult diapers, faded. "The last time I saw you, you threatened to sic your aunt Lou on me if I came within ten miles of you," he said. "And when I tried to stop you from pulling out of the parking lot, you ran over my foot."

I glared at him. "I did *not* run over your foot!"

"What? You thought I was faking? I couldn't put

68

weight on it for a week. I could have used a little compassion after what I went through," he added.

"After what *you* went through? What about *me*? I'm the one who got the call that my husband had fallen through the floor of a burning building and had been rushed to the ER. I'm the one who almost wrecked my car speeding to the hospital, not knowing if you were seriously injured or near death."

"But I didn't die. I just banged up my shoulder. You could have at least hung around long enough to help me out, instead of throwing your suitcases in your car, then running over my foot!"

I would never admit that I had wanted him to realize how much he needed me so he'd leave the fire department. My plan hadn't worked. "*If* I ran over your foot, I didn't mean to."

"Even the guys at the station felt bad for me."

"I was angry as hell at the time, okay? Stark fear has a way of doing that to you." We stared at each other. I suddenly recalled him standing in the parking lot that day, yelping as I backed away and accusing me of running over his foot. It hadn't been humorous then, but now I choked back a sudden laugh.

"You think that's funny?" he said, although he looked amused as well.

I realized I was a little tipsy. "I'm really sorry, Jay. I had no idea."

"Thank you for your apology, Katie. It only took you five and a half months."

"You've been waiting all this time for *me* to apologize to *you*?" I said in disbelief.

Someone accidentally bumped me from behind, and I struggled to stay atop my stiletto heels. Jay caught me. His hand at my waist sent shivers through me.

"Are you okay?"

"Fine," I said. But I wasn't fine. I was dizzy, and I needed food. Any idiot knows you shouldn't drink on an empty stomach. Plus my feet hurt. I should have examined my own head for buying four-inch whore heels to begin with. How was I supposed to make my grand exit and leave Jay wanting me if I couldn't walk?

I searched the crowd, which had doubled in size in a matter of minutes. "I have to find Mona," I said.

"You'll never make it across the room in those high heels, Katie-Lee. You'll fall flat on your face, and everybody will see your undies."

This was my cue. I slapped my hand over my mouth. "Uh-oh," I said.

Jay met my gaze. "Don't tell me you're not wearing panties."

"It's a thong," I whispered conspiratorially, and had the pleasure of watching his jaw go slack.

"Oh, hell," he said.

Our gazes locked, and I was pretty sure I caught a look of unbridled desire in his eyes. But the moment was ruined when my stomach growled so loudly that a woman nearby turned and looked at me as if I had just passed gas. I was on the verge of intoxication, and if I didn't eat soon, I was going to pass out. "I have to leave now," I said, feeling less like a temptress and more like Wimp-Woman. "I don't feel so great."

I must've sounded desperate, because Jay suddenly looked concerned. "I'll take you wherever you want to go. My SUV is close by."

Mona was nowhere to be seen. "I guess so," I said. I took a deep breath and tucked my arm through his to steady myself.

"Can you make it to the door?" he asked.

I nodded, and we moved slowly in that direction. A waiter paused and offered us hors d'oeuvres from a tray. I grabbed a fistful of cheese cubes and ignored the stunned look on his face.

At the door, I glanced over my shoulder, searching the crowd once more. I found Mona and caught her eye. She looked from me to Jay and back at me, then gave me the thumbs-up sign. Behind her, my mother and aunt were grinning and doing high fives.

A blast of hot air hit me as Jay and I stepped outside. True to his word, we didn't have far to walk.

Inside his black SUV, he turned the air on high. I aimed a vent at my face and wolfed down the cheese.

Jay watched me. "You must be really hungry." He reached into the backseat and handed me a bottle of water.

I took a long drink. "I'm okay now," I said.

"Great." He smiled.

I smiled back.

71

He put the gear into drive. "Where to, Katie?" he asked. "Your place or mine?"

When I opened my eyes, it was morning and I was in Jay's bed, naked as the day I was born. *Hell's bells!* I'd gone and slept with my soon-to-be-ex-husband! I'd let a little bit of champagne and a whole lot of lust override good common sense.

I sat bolt upright in the bed. The sun was bright coming through the twelve-foot windows of the loft. I checked the alarm clock. *Eight thirty!* I tried to think. Mr. Lewey was due in at nine. I specifically remembered him calling on Friday, asking if he could see me.

I heard the shower running in the bathroom and scrambled from the bed. I had no desire to face Jay Rush, not after how we'd spent the evening. I'm almost sure some of what we did was still illegal in certain states.

I yanked my dress from the floor, pulled it over my head, and searched for my thong. Where the hell was my thong? I checked the covers and looked beneath the bed, then raced from the room, trying to make as little sound as possible.

The place looked much the same as it had when I'd lived there. The building had once served as a mill and was converted to lofts in the late nineties. The brick walls, wood floors, and twenty-foot ceilings, not to mention Jay's masculine furniture, had given the place a stark look that I'd softened with slipcovers, shaggy rugs, and window treatments after I'd moved in.

I did not see my thong. My high heels were still lying beside the front door, where I'd kicked them off when I'd come through the night before; beside them lay my small evening bag. I grabbed both.

Damn, damn, damn! Where was my thong? I started for the bedroom once again, only to hear Jay shut off the shower. I did an about-face and ran on tiptoes to the front door. I turned the dead bolt, slid the chain free, and ran out.

Once I was on the sidewalk out front, it hit me: I had no cell phone to call a cab. I slipped on my stilettos and started down the sidewalk as quickly as I could. In the parking lot next to the building, I saw a woman and a young girl getting out of a car. I hurried over.

I didn't recognize the woman, but she could have been a new tenant. "Excuse me," I said, noting her arched brows and the way she pulled her daughter closer as I neared them. "Do you happen to have a cell phone on you?"

The woman hesitated.

"Mommy, is that lady a hooker?" the little girl asked.

The woman turned stricken eyes to her daughter. "Where did you learn that word?" she demanded. "That is *not* a word we use in our family."

"I'm just a regular person," I said, "who needs to make a quick phone call."

Still eyeing me dubiously, the woman reached into

her purse and pulled out a cell phone. I dialed the office and prayed Mona would have arrived by now. She picked up on the second ring. "It's me," I said. "I don't have time to explain, but I'm outside Jay's place. I need a cab, fast. Mr. Lewey is coming in at nine."

For once Mona didn't question me. I gave her the address. "Tell the driver to pull into the parking lot next to the building. Tell him not to leave if he doesn't see me right away. I'll be hiding behind the building, but I'll watch for him." I started to hang up. "Oh, one more thing," I added quickly. "If you can get your hands on a pair of clean underwear, I'd appreciate it. I've lost mine." But Mona had already hung up.

I heard a gasp. The woman had her hands pressed against her daughter's ears. "This is a respectable neighborhood," she hissed.

"It's not what you think," I said.

She yanked the phone from my hand and all but dragged her daughter away as quickly as possible.

I hid behind the building, hoping and praying the cab would arrive quickly. I should *never* have gone to Jay's place to begin with. I was a weak woman, an embarrassment to women everywhere. All Jay'd had to do was nuzzle the back of my neck, and I'd been a goner. I covered my eyes, but it didn't block the memory of me pulling off my thong and dangling it in his face.

I'd lost control. I recalled tugging the front of his shirt from his jeans. There'd been no stopping me. Not that Jay had tried. We'd barely made it to the bedroom before he had me out of my dress. Our lips had remained fused together, even as he'd hovered over me, as he sank into me, and I'd felt my body shiver and my liver quiver at the fierce pleasure. Our lovemaking had been fast and furious, two people answering a desperate mutual need. Nothing else mattered.

It wasn't until later, when we'd made love a second time and the urgency had been replaced by long, lingering kisses and gentle explorations, that I realized Jay Rush still had the master key to my heart.

My first mistake had been going to the grand opening to begin with. I should have called my mother and pretended to have Lyme disease. Now I was forced to face the absolute truth that I was still as crazy about Jay as I'd been the day I married him. Nothing had changed in the six months we'd been apart. I was going to have to go through the whole heartbreak thing again.

As I waited for the cab, I worked on my multiplication tables.

For once, luck seemed to be with me; the cab arrived in ten minutes. Jay's car had not left the parking lot, and if he'd come out to look for me, I hadn't seen him from my vantage point. I darted toward the cab as fast as I could, waving both hands in the air so the driver wouldn't miss me. As if he could. I yanked the door open, lost my footing, and all but tumbled into the backseat.

"Holy mother of God!" the man said in a thick Italian accent. "You're not wearing underwear."

I blushed so hard that I was certain I'd singed my

eyebrows. I slammed the door and tried to tuck my dress under me as I recalled what Mona had said about what went on in the backseats of cabs. I was too embarrassed to meet the driver's gaze, but I glanced at his photo near the meter and saw that his name was Tony. "Um, Tony, I'm in a really big hurry," I said.

He gunned the engine and squealed from the parking lot, sending me flying across the backseat again. I was aware of him darting looks in the rearview mirror, from which a crucifix dangled. "Does your father know what you're doing?" he asked.

"Excuse me?"

"This is no life for a pretty girl like you."

"I'm not a hooker, if that's what you're thinking. I'm a professional in the business of helping people, um, heal." I'm not sure why I felt it necessary to defend myself to a perfect stranger, but the crucifix was staring me in the face.

"Oh, so you're telling me you're a nurse? Well, that's some uniform you have there, young lady."

I ignored him.

"I have a daughter your age," he said. As he sped down the street, holding the steering wheel with one hand, he whipped out his wallet with the other. "This is her picture."

She had her father's nose. "She's very attractive," I lied. With his thumb, Tony flipped the picture, and I found myself looking at the fattest baby I'd ever seen. He had his mother's nose.

"My grandson, Antonio," he said. "Named after me, of course," he added proudly. "They call him Tony Number Two. There is nothing more precious than a grandchild. You should get married and give your poor mother grandchildren before you're all used up like a bar of hand soap."

"Look, I appreciate your concern, Tony, but I need to get to my office." I sat back in the seat, crossed my arms, and stared out the window. Tony obviously got the message, because he kept quiet the rest of the way.

By the time we arrived, I'd managed to repair my hair with the plastic hair pick in my purse.

I pulled out my cash, paid Tony, and hurried from the cab. I tried to ignore the stares of those waiting beside me for the elevator. When I stepped out on the fourth floor, I froze. Down the hall, people spilled from my reception room, sipping coffee and eating pastries.

Oh, crap! How could I have forgotten Open House Day, which fell on the first Monday of each month? Mona had come up with the idea in the hope of building my practice and ultimately making me famous. There was little I could say, since she paid for the advertisement as well as the caterer. Plus I didn't want to hurt her feelings, even though the event hadn't produced a single new patient. It had, instead, turned into a social event for building employees and residents from a nearby retirement center, who were bused in.

More stares. I entered my office and stepped up to Mona's desk. "I have a little problem."

"No, you have a *big* problem," Mona said. "Screwy Lewey freaked out when he saw all these people. He's hiding in the bathroom. I thought he was just afraid of elevators."

There was no time to admonish Mona for the remark, and it would have been unethical to discuss Mr. Lewey's fears. With his claustrophobia, he would have panicked in a tight crowd of people. "I need a clean outfit," I said. "Can you do that?"

She held out her hand. "House key?"

I pulled it from my purse and dropped it into her palm. "Also, clean underwear. I lost the thong."

Mona gave me a look. "Slut," she whispered.

I crossed the reception room, pausing to sign a couple of autographs. In Mona's attempt to draw in new patients, she handed out goody bags stuffed with pens, notepads, and miniature boxes of chocolates. Also included were brochures on mental health, my business card, and a glossy eight-by-ten of me sitting in my wingback chair, holding a clipboard. Below my picture were the words "Your Compassionate Friend." I scribbled my name and hurried down the hall.

I tapped on the bathroom door. "Mr. Lewey, it's me, Kate. Are you okay?"

"No, I'm *not* okay," he said. "I'm hyperventilating, and I'm not coming out until those people leave."

I could hear the anxiety in his voice, but I knew the crowd wouldn't leave until they'd eaten every last doughnut and croissant. Some of the seniors would ask for to-go bags.

"Please let me in, Mr. Lewey," I said.

"Are you alone?"

"Scout's honor."

The lock clicked, and he peered through the slit. He did a double take at my dress. "How come you're dressed like a call girl?"

"Just let me in, okay?"

He stepped back. I scooted inside, and he slammed the door behind me and locked it again.

"I shouldn't have scheduled you for this morning," I said. "I forgot we'd have visitors."

He was trembling. "This is going to set me way back."

"It doesn't have to, Mr. Lewey. Do you think you could follow me to my office?"

He put the toilet lid down and sat. "No way am I going out there."

"Perhaps if we tried a deep-breathing exercise," I suggested.

"How do you expect me to relax when I'm sitting on a toilet and you're wearing that dress?"

"This will be an excellent learning tool for you, Mr. Lewey. It is important for you to know that you can call on the skills you've learned, no matter where you are."

He seemed to be considering it, when a sharp knock on the bathroom door startled me and made him jump.

"Don't let anyone in here!" he yelled.

Mona called out from the other side. I cracked open the door. "What are you guys doing in there?" she said.

"We're in the middle of a session."

Mona smacked her forehead. "Silly me. I should have known that." She leaned closer and whispered, "Jay's out front. He said he had something you'd want." Mona sighed. "I have to tell you, I got goose pimples just thinking about it."

I hoped Jay had my thong. "Mr. Lewey, I have to step out for a minute," I said. "Mona will guard the door while I'm gone. Just work on your breathing techniques."

I spied Jay eating a chocolate éclair and talking to one of the residents of the retirement home. I motioned him toward my office, and he stepped inside. I caught the scent of his aftershave, and my stomach did a flip-flop. "I'm in the middle of a session," I said, trying to control my breathing.

"You're holding a session in the bathroom in *that* dress?" He popped the last of the éclair in his mouth.

I watched him chew and had images of that mouth kissing my neck, my eyelids, and my breasts. I had images of those lips pressed inside my thighs. I tried to reel in my thoughts. "Did I happen to leave anything at your place?"

"Why did you run out on me, Katie? I didn't hear the fire alarm go off."

The look in his eyes made my heart skip a beat. "It's complicated."

"You *make* it complicated." He reached into the pocket of his jeans and pulled out my thong.

I snatched it from him and tried to slip it on discreetly. "I have to get back now." I put my hand on the doorknob.

He covered my hand with his. "Call me."

"Yeah, okay."

"I'm serious, Katie. We need to talk." He pulled a pen from his pocket, took my hand, and wrote a phone number on my open palm.

My breath caught in the back of my throat as I noted the way his dark hair fell against his forehead, as I recalled running my fingers through it, smelling the scent of his shampoo.

"My cell number, in case you've forgotten it," he said. He raised my palm to his face and pressed his lips against it. I bit my bottom lip to keep from sighing in pleasure.

chapter 5

······························

It was well past lunchtime, and I'd seen three patients. Thanks to Mona's housekeeper, I was finally dressed appropriately and wearing regular panties. With an hour to kill until my next patient, I decided to treat Mona to lunch at the sandwich shop downstairs. She wasn't at her desk, so I hurried down the hall, thinking I might find her in the kitchenette.

I paused at the doorway. Sitting in a chair at the table was a middle-aged woman reading a magazine. Her feet were propped on another chair, where a much younger woman in a white lab coat was applying polish to the woman's toenails.

The girl looked up and smiled. "You must be Dr. Holly."

I nodded. "Have we met?"

"I'm Nancy. I used to be the manicurist at the salon downstairs. I don't remember seeing you. Mona said you don't get many manicures."

I looked at the woman in the chair.

"I'm Ida," she said, glancing at me from over her magazine.

"Mona said it would be okay if I used the kitchen until I find another job," Nancy said.

She couldn't have been more than eighteen or nineteen. "Where is Mona, by the way?" I asked.

"She's having lunch with her boyfriend. I told her I would answer the phone while she was out." Nancy had barely gotten the words out of her mouth before the phone rang on Mona's desk. "Oops, there it is." She hurried from the room.

"So you're a psychologist, eh?" Ida said.

I nodded and turned to go.

"Maybe you could give me your opinion."

I knew what was coming. The minute people discovered I was a psychologist, they proceeded to tell me about some friend or family member who had always acted odd, and I was expected to diagnose that person on the spot. "I doubt I can help you," I said.

"It's about Nancy," Ida said as though she hadn't heard me.

"I've just met her," I said. "I don't know anything about her."

"Well, I'm concerned. I don't want to hurt her feelings, but I think this toenail polish has too much orange in it. What do you think?"

"I brought you a sandwich," Mona said, only minutes before my next patient was due to arrive. I motioned her inside my office and told her to close the door.

"Why do we have a nail salon in the kitchen?" I asked.

"Nancy's boss fired her," Mona whispered. "Said she wasn't bringing in enough customers," she added.

"How many laws are we breaking, since we don't actually have a license to operate a nail salon?" I asked.

"It's only temporary. Till Nancy finds a job. She doesn't want to lose her regular customers in the meantime. Plus it works to our advantage, on account of I've come up with this great marketing plan."

I tried to hold my fear at bay. "What marketing plan?"

"For the next two weeks, all new patients get a free manicure. The ad is in today's paper. There's a coupon."

I just looked at her. "Mona, does it strike you as odd that none of the other businesses in this building offer open houses or coupons for manicures?"

"Kate, as your publicist, I need to remind you: Trust me." She checked her wristwatch. "You'd better eat that sandwich fast. Your next appointment will be here any minute." She excused herself and headed toward the restroom.

The phone rang, and I answered it.

"I need to speak to Dr. Holly," a male voice said.

"This is Dr. Holly."

"You're a nuisance," he said. "A troublemaker," he added. "I don't like troublemakers."

I noticed he had a lisp. "Who is this?" I asked.

"You don't need to know my name. Stop making trouble, and I won't make trouble for you."

He hung up, and I stared at the phone.

"What's wrong?" Mona asked when she came out of the bathroom a few minutes later. I realized I was still holding the phone. I could feel my mouth hanging open.

I repeated what the man had said. Mona and I simply stared at each other, perplexed frowns on our faces. It suddenly hit me. "I'll bet you anything he's a member of Bitsy Stout's church. They're all a bunch of nutcases. Bitsy put him up to it to scare me." I told Mona about my statue.

"He threatened you," Mona said. "You should call the police."

"I can't prove anything," I told her. "I don't even know his name."

"Would you recognize his voice again if you heard it?"

I thought about the lisp. "Yeah."

Mona shook her head. "I don't like this, Kate. You don't want some crazy religious fanatic coming after you. Watch your back."

I gave a mental sigh. Like I didn't have enough to think about these days, I thought.

According to the DSM—the *Diagnostic and Statistical Manual of Mental Disorders*, published by the American Psychiatric Association—Cynthia Reed suffered from body dysmorphia. To put it plainly, she imagined grotesque physical defects and spent much of her time and money on plastic surgery. At thirty, she had already been nipped, tucked, plumped, lifted, and suctioned, and although the results had made her prettier in some ways, I was concerned. A lot of body dysmorphics continue to have enough work done that they end up looking odd.

I'd only recently begun seeing Cynthia, but she had agreed not to have any body parts changed or rearranged without discussing it with me beforehand. Which was why I was more than a little disappointed when Mona slipped into my office to announce Cynthia's arrival and inform me that she'd had another procedure.

"Holy cow," Mona whispered. "She's had her lips plumped again. If they get any bigger, she'll be able to give blow jobs from across the room."

I should have known something was up. Cynthia had cancelled her appointments two weeks in a row. The first time was allegedly to take her ailing mother to the doctor. "Did you say anything to her?" I asked.

Mona shook her head. "What? You think I'm that insensitive?"

When Cynthia sat down in my office, I pretended not to notice her lips. She was an advertising executive and was always dressed to the nines. "How's your mother?" I asked.

She gave me a funny look, as if she expected me to reprimand her for falling off the plastic surgery wagon. "She's better," Cynthia said. "It was her blood pressure. Her cholesterol was high. She has gained thirty pounds in the last couple of years, and it's causing health problems. Dad is furious with her, of course."

Cynthia's father was a health nut and had been for years. He was obsessive—measuring and weighing his food, keeping exercise journals. And he was highly critical of Cynthia's mother and, I suspected, Cynthia as well. Although Cynthia resented the constant tension when she visited, there was a part of her that didn't want to disappoint her father and risk losing his love.

"I am so angry with my father for making Mom feel bad about herself," Cynthia said. "I have to bite my tongue not to say anything."

"What would happen if you or your mother told him how you felt?"

"He'd get mad."

"What does he do when he gets mad?"

"He pouts. He goes hours, days, weeks without saying anything."

I nodded. I don't like pouting. It creates tension and

prolongs issues that need to be aired and solved. I suspected Cynthia's father, who was obviously a control freak, gained a certain amount of control through his pouting. "What would happen if you and your mother ignored the pouting?"

"It's hard to ignore," Cynthia said.

"But suppose you tried. Suppose you and your mother went shopping or out to lunch and left him alone to pout?"

She seemed to think about it. Finally she smiled. "There'd be nobody around to watch him do it. I guess it would be a drag for him, huh?"

"It would definitely take the fun out of it," I said, smiling too. "It's hard to be a really good pouter without an audience."

Her smile faded, and she looked thoughtful. "I just wish he'd stop."

"Why should he, when it gets him what he wants?" I asked. "When he has a wife and daughter who go to so much trouble to win his approval?"

Cynthia averted her gaze. She folded her arms and sat quietly. It appeared as though she was trying to hug herself, to provide the comfort and closeness and, especially, the acceptance she'd probably never gotten from her father.

It amazes me how many well-meaning parents screw up their kids' lives. If it weren't for poor parenting, I'd be out of business. I dreaded having kids, because I knew I'd screw up their lives just like my mother had screwed up mine. It's like a torch that must be passed from generation to generation.

"He has made me feel bad about myself for a long time," Cynthia finally said. "When I was a little girl, I was chubby. He called me—" She reached for a tissue and dabbed her eyes. "He called me Doodlebug. Do you know what doodlebugs look like? They roll up into fat little balls when they're scared. I hate him for making me feel like a fat bug," she added. "He *still* calls me Doodlebug, and he knows I hate it."

I just nodded.

"And you know what's worse? He used to have a weight problem when he was younger. Who does he think he is, making people feel fat? Not just fat," she said, "but not good enough. I've felt that way my entire life." Her bottom lip trembled. "I hate feeling bad about myself."

"Especially when you have so much going for you," I pointed out. "You have a great career. You own a lovely home, and—"

"And I have wonderful friends who like and respect me," she added. "Most men find me very attractive."

"You *are* very attractive," I said, although I feared that one or two more times under the knife would cut away her nicest features. But the only person who could convince Cynthia she was good enough, inside and out, was Cynthia.

This idea is so elementary that I don't know why everybody, including me, doesn't get it. No, we have to drag ourselves through a mire of angst in order to figure it out.

Cynthia was probably going to have to confront her father to get validation of her feelings before she could begin to heal.

"Have you ever thought of telling your father how you feel?" I asked.

"Many times," she said. "But I can never work up the nerve. Plus—" She paused again and swiped at more tears. "It would be painful. And when I'm in pain, I get angry. Really angry. I'm afraid I would lose control."

"Perhaps you could practice by writing down what you'd like to say to him. Sometimes writing things down helps ease the pain and anger," I added.

She nodded, but the tears continued to fall. There are times when it's best to keep quiet and let people cry. So I let Cynthia cry, and I made sure she had fresh tissues when she needed them.

It's not easy for me to watch people go through pain. Nor is it easy for me to remain professionally detached. But it's the only way I can help them. If I allow myself to get mired in their suffering, I'll go under with them. Somebody has to stand onshore ready to throw the life preserver.

My job could really depress me if I let it. I guess that's why some therapists become cynical or make bad jokes. That's why I was so familiar with the protective shield Jack Hix used against his nagging wife.

In my mind, I had a special closet filled with nooks

and crannies, and that's where I stuffed all the really bad crap I heard. I couldn't afford to carry it around with me on a daily basis. I'd had to teach some of my more troubled patients to do the same thing between sessions so that they could carry on their lives outside my office.

Finally Cynthia's tears subsided. I'll admit I was impressed. Most women end up with mascara running down their faces. Cynthia's mascara was obviously waterproof.

"How are you feeling?" I asked.

"Much better," she said. "I didn't realize I was so hurt."

"I'm glad you were able to get some of it out," I said gently.

I reached for my appointment book. Cynthia had spent so much time crying that her session had ended. But it was just as well: I suspected she had been through enough for one day.

"Do you think you could come back on Friday?" I asked.

She looked surprised. "So soon?"

I nodded. I figured that since Cynthia was in touch with all her pain, it would be best to get her back in as soon as possible, or she might end up with a bad nose job. We agreed on a time. "I'm going to give you some homework," I said. "I'd like for you to write a letter to your father and bring it with you next time."

She looked alarmed. "And say what?"

"Tell him how you feel. How you've felt for most of your life," I added.

She nodded thoughtfully. She started to get up. "Um, I was wondering—" She sniffed. "I saw the coupon in the newspaper for the free manicure. Is that for new patients only? I could really use a good manicure."

"Jay called," Mona said after I'd seen my last patient of the day, "and your mom called twice. She wants to throw a party for you and Jay, now that the two of you are back together."

"Jay and I aren't back together!"

"Oh, so I'm supposed to tell your mother you were just using him for sex?"

It figured that my mother would want to know what was going on after seeing Jay and me leave the party together. "I *wasn't* using him for sex," I said.

"Oh." Mona paused. "So what *were* you doing?"

"How the hell do I know what I was doing?" I said.

"Isn't that sort of your specialty? To know why people do the things they do?" she added.

"I can't be my own therapist!" I went inside my office and closed the door. I sat at my desk and counted my pens. Mona knocked. I didn't say anything. She opened the door anyway.

"Boy, are you in denial," she said.

"I'm not in denial."

"You need to talk to Bubba-Bear."

"Do not pull out that bear!" I said when Mona made a move to grab him.

"Admit it, then. You're in denial."

"I'm not!"

She looked thoughtful. "Then are you disassociating?"

"What?"

"I heard Dr. Phil use that word."

"You need to stop taping his show, and no, I'm not disassociating."

"Would you know it if you were?" she asked. "Or would it take another therapist to tell you?"

"Maybe I'm just having a bad day because I didn't get much sleep last night, and I lost my underwear. How would you like it if you had to come to work without underwear?"

It was then that I noticed Nancy, the manicurist, standing in the doorway, her mouth agape.

"I just wanted to let you know I'm leaving for the day," she said, "and to tell you that the lady with the fat lips really enjoyed having her nails done. I'm going to give her a pedicure on Friday."

Mona looked annoyed. "That's supposed to be for new patients only, Kate."

"Yeah, but I'm the boss," I said, "and if Cynthia wants a pedicure on Friday, then she gets one."

Nancy mumbled something and hurried out.

"Fine," Mona said, getting testy. "We'll give everybody a free manicure. We'll have free manicures on Open House Day, how's that? We'll even offer them during the mental health fair."

I just looked at her. Some months back, Mona had come up with the idea to hold a mental health fair, despite my many attempts to discourage her. Just thinking what she might do filled me with a sense of dread. "I don't want a mental health fair."

"It'll be good for you. It'll take your mind off you-know-who."

Mona had chosen to have the fair on the same Friday that my divorce was to become final. "Where are you going to hold a fair, Mona? In the parking lot?"

"Yes, and I've already made it okay with many of the building tenants and asked them to pass the word."

"It's going to be very inconvenient for a lot of people."

"They'll get over it once they see all the free food and drinks, not to mention a live band. And just think, by the time it's over, everybody will know who you are."

That's what I was afraid of.

"Like I said before, Kate, you're going to have to trust me. I've got your career all mapped out. One day you'll thank me."

I wondered what it would be like to have a normal family and a normal best friend. I heard the door to the reception room open, and a moment later a gorgeous hunk of a man stood in my doorway. He was young, with longish blond hair, and looked as though he belonged on the cover of *GQ*. I hoped he was a new patient who would take years to heal.

"Liam, what a surprise!" Mona said, giving him a huge smile.

I tried to hide my disappointment.

"I came by to invite you to dinner," he said.

"Oh, that's so sweet." Mona introduced us.

He smiled, hurried to my desk, and reached across to shake my hand. "You're really young to be a psychologist," he said.

He flashed me the dimples Mona had mentioned so many times. Now I understood why she couldn't bear the thought of getting naked in front of him. "I'm the same age as Mona," I said for lack of anything more interesting to say.

"You're only twenty-eight, and you already have your own practice" he said. "That's impressive."

I looked at Mona, who cut her eyes at me. "Well, you kids enjoy your evening," I said. They started out the door. "And, Mona?" She paused and stuck her head through the doorway. "Don't stay out past your curfew."

With my list of wholesome foods in hand, I drove to the grocery store and loaded my cart with fresh fruits and vegetables: cauliflower, broccoli, baby carrots, nice purplish asparagus spears that were ridiculously overpriced, and plump ripe tomatoes. I added bananas, a container of giant strawberries, Red Delicious apples, and a plastic bag filled with seedless grapes.

I found a box of cereal that promised to lower my cholesterol, prevent heart disease and cancer, and provide me with enough nutrients that I would never again have to worry about taking my multivitamin tablet before I left for the office.

At the meat counter, I turned my nose up at the steaks and tossed in a pack of boneless, skinless chicken breasts.

I bought skim milk, whole wheat bread, and olive oil that wore a seal of approval from the American Heart Association. I figured that at this rate, I was going to live until age 110.

I headed toward the front of the store to check out and skidded to a dead halt when I saw the "buy one, get one free" offer for Ben & Jerry's ice cream. I gave myself a mental smack on the forehead. What was I thinking!

It hadn't occurred to me that the healthy new diet and lifestyle I'd planned might be a little extreme. Extremes don't work, especially when it comes to diet and exercise. You can have the best intentions, but if you're not at all flexible, you can sabotage your best efforts and set yourself up for one huge failure. Which leads only to low self-esteem, of course, and maybe even an eating disorder, I reminded myself.

There are times when it helps to be an expert in human behavior. I promptly turned my cart around and headed for the freezer section.

I arrived home to find the word "Jezebel" painted on my front door, which meant that either Bitsy Stout or her crazy friend with the lisp had paid a visit. And that really annoyed me, because I knew I had to take some kind of action, but I didn't know what *kind* of action.

And *that* annoyed me further because I was hungry, and I had two pints of Ben & Jerry's chocolate fudge in my grocery bag, calling out to me.

Fortunately I was hit with such a brilliant thought that I surprised even myself. I unlocked my door and carried in my groceries, then went to the upstairs guest room, where I still had boxes to unpack. It took ten minutes of devoted searching before I found my camera. Luckily there was still film left.

I hurried downstairs and out the front door. I knew Bitsy was watching, which was why I made a production of taking pictures, treating it like a crime scene. Bitsy was probably gnawing her bottom lip and wondering what I was going to do next. She would probably wait until it was dark to wash the paint off. She'd want to know that I was asleep.

With my proof caught on film, I turned toward Bitsy's house and gave her the finger. It wasn't my best moment, but it felt good. Sometimes you just have to do what feels really good.

By the time I unloaded my groceries, I was too tired to cook; plus I'd forgotten to buy a vegetable steamer. I changed clothes and made myself a bowl of soup. I chose vegetable soup in keeping with my new eating plan. When the phone rang, I ignored it.

My mother's voice came on the answering machine. "Kate, pick up. I know you're there." A long pause. "Kate, I've been thinking about you and Jay. I just have one word of advice for you."

I pressed my fingers to my ears so that I didn't have to hear it. I realized I was acting as if I were four years old, but I didn't care. I was in crisis. It felt good to act four years old. Just as it had felt good to flip off Bitsy Stout.

The answering machine beeped, and my mother was gone.

I was finishing up my soup when the phone rang again.

Jay's voice came on. "We need to talk, Katie. Please pick up the phone."

I sighed. Why did everybody just assume I was spending a dull night at home? I really did need to reinvent myself.

"Katie, we need to talk," Jay said.

"It's been almost six months, you idiot," I muttered. "I have nothing to say to you."

"Katie, I know you think I'm an idiot for not calling in almost six months," Jay said, "but I really think it's time we discussed a few things. You've got my number, so call me, okay?"

He hung up.

I tried not to think of how we'd spent the previous night; of how, while I was lying on my stomach in his bed, he'd run his tongue down the length of my spine and I'd shivered so hard, my teeth had rattled.

I washed my dirty dishes. Instead of falling on the couch as I would normally have done, I decided to take a walk so it would look good on my progress sheet. I had gone only a couple of blocks before I realized a dog was following me, some kind of terrier mixed with something I didn't recognize. I ignored it, even when it caught up with me and managed to meet my stride, despite its stubby legs.

"Go away," I said, but when I turned back for home, the dog followed. There was no collar, which meant the animal was probably a stray, but a well-fed stray, since its belly was plenty big enough. He or she had probably been mooching off my neighbors.

The dog followed me to my front door, but I continued to ignore it, mainly because I loved animals and could easily get sucked in by soft brown eyes. I let myself in and locked the door behind me. I grabbed a pint of Ben & Jerry's and a spoon, turned on The Movie Channel, and sat on the sofa. I was well into both the ice cream and the movie plot when I decided to check on the dog. He was curled on my stoop.

The phone rang, and I picked up. No answer, but I could hear someone breathing. "I know who this is," I said, "and I expect you to wash that stupid paint off my door or I'm going to take legal action." I slammed down the phone.

The movie ended, and I went to bed, thankful to have the day behind me. I awoke sometime later to the crash of thunder, and pouring rain. I remembered the dog and hurried downstairs. I cracked my front door open and saw the animal pressed against it, wet and shivering.

Finally I let him in. His tail wagged as he gazed up at

me like I was his new best friend. "Don't get your hopes up," I said, using my sternest voice. "You're only staying for the night." I studied him closely. "I'll bet you're hungry."

I opened a can of tuna fish and watched him devour it. I put water into a bowl and carried it to my laundry room. He followed and drank the water while I grabbed an old towel and put it on the floor. "Okay, this is where you'll sleep," I said, pointing. The dog immediately curled up on the towel. I could almost swear he smiled at me.

"Good night," I said. I paused and added, "Mike." He looked like he should be named Mike.

I only hoped Mike didn't have fleas.

Candles flickered around the bed. *Hundreds of them, in an assortment of sizes and shapes, their flames repeated and made brighter by surrounding mirrors. They flickered on the sills of tall leaded-glass windows, adding a feeling of warmth and intimacy to the room, despite the great storm outside, beating against the castle.*

Castle? I had no idea what I was doing in a castle. I didn't even know anyone who owned a castle.

I gazed down at Jay, tanned and muscular and naked against white satin sheets. His blue eyes caressed my face as I leaned over him and nuzzled the dark hair on his chest. I splayed my fingers and watched the silken hairs curl around them, and I tongued one nipple. Jay's breath was warm on my cheek and neck.

I reached below, encircled him with my hand, found him hard.

"I love you, Katie," he said. "I'll quit the fire department. I'll go to work for Uncle Bump."

I rose slightly, guided Jay to my heat, and lowered my body. My head fell back as he filled me exquisitely. Our sighs mingled and hovered in the air, and Jay cupped my hips tightly, digging his nails deep in my flesh until I cried out. I rode him hard and the heat rose in my belly, hotter and hotter until . . .

A clap of thunder woke me, and I sat bolt upright in the bed. It was dark. I felt the pillow beside me and was not surprised to find myself alone. Just another dream, one of many I'd had since leaving Jay.

They always left me sad, but I preferred them to some of the other dreams I had. The bad ones. Those dreams consisted of tall burning buildings. Skyscrapers that loomed so high, they poked through the clouds. And like an idiot, I always found myself climbing the stairs to the top, even though I knew I was headed for disaster. I hated those dreams, but they'd been with me for more than twenty years.

I reached to turn on the lamp beside my bed, but nothing happened. Obviously I'd lost power. I opened the drawer of my night table and pulled out a flashlight. I shone it on my battery-powered alarm clock. Five a.m.

I got out of bed and looked out the window. Lightning flashed, followed closely by more thunder. The rain fell in sheets, and I was thankful I'd brought Mike the stray inside. I imagined him huddled and trembling from the noise of the storm.

Still holding my flashlight, I carefully picked my way downstairs. I opened the door to the laundry room and found Mike standing there, his brown eyes pleading. "What is it, boy?"

He grunted. I knelt on the floor, and my hand brushed something small and warm. It wiggled. I gave a shudder of horror, thinking I had a mouse in my laundry room. Even worse, I'd touched it! I had an attack of heebie-jeebies and came to my feet so fast that I made myself dizzy. Quickly, I shined the light on the floor. Holy hell, it was a puppy! Nearby, there were three more just like it.

"You're not a Mike," I said. "You're a girl! And you forgot to mention you were pregnant!"

Despite her straining, she licked my foot. I bent over and stroked her head. "I hope you know what you're doing, because I'm clueless."

I hurried to the kitchen and dialed Mona. She answered sleepily. "There's a dog in my laundry room having puppies," I blurted, "and I don't know what to do."

"Huh? When did you get a dog?"

I gave Mona a brief summary of how I'd ended up with a stray. "I should probably put the puppies on a towel or something, but I'm scared to pick them up. Plus my power is out."

"Let me wake Mrs. Perez," Mona said. "I'll call you back."

I felt relieved as I hung up. Mrs. Perez was Mona's housekeeper and the most capable woman I knew. I'd seen her get a red wine stain out of Mona's white carpet.

The phone rang ten minutes later. "Mrs. Perez will be there as soon as she can," Mona said, "but it'll take longer in this weather. She said you don't need to do anything; the mama dog will know what to do. Oh, and try to stay out of the dog's way so you don't make her nervous. I'll be over after I shower."

I hated that Mrs. Perez had to drive in bad weather, but I feared there would be a glitch in one of the puppy births, and I wouldn't know how to help. "Could you please grab a can of dog food on the way over?" I asked Mona. "All I have is tuna fish."

I hung up and made my way to the laundry room door, but didn't go in. I aimed the flashlight at Mike. She was busy licking the puppy she'd just expelled. "You're doing great," I said, thinking I should prod her on. I gave her a thumbs-up. Then, I paced the kitchen and waited.

chapter 6

·····················

Mrs. Perez arrived an hour later carrying a box, a heating pad, a stack of newspapers, and a couple of towels. The storm had blown over, and power had been restored. Mike had delivered yet another puppy. I'd managed to take a quick shower and put on minimal makeup, but I was still in my bathrobe.

"Who painted your front door?" Mrs. Perez asked as she looked in on Mike, who seemed to be resting, her puppies still scattered about.

I gave a mental sigh. Obviously Bitsy had not taken my warning seriously. "My neighbor doesn't like me," I said.

Mrs. Perez immediately prepared the box, putting the heating pad beneath the towels and covering it all with newspaper. "You'll want to keep the area warm for the puppies," she said. I followed her inside the laundry room, where she placed the box in a corner to avoid drafts. I plugged in the heating pad as she petted Mike, then carefully placed the puppies in the box.

Mike didn't look concerned that Mrs. Perez was handling her newborns. She walked to her water bowl and began lapping greedily before heading to the back door. I let her out, and she was quick to do her business and come right back.

"I don't know if she's finished having her litter, so we should stay out of her way," Mrs. Perez said as Mike climbed in the box and began sniffing and nuzzling her new family as though wanting to make sure each was healthy and perfectly formed. We went back into the kitchen, and I poured Mrs. Perez a cup of coffee.

"You'll need to change the newspapers when they get soiled," she said. "The mama must be fed several times a day so she'll have plenty of milk for her babies."

"How do you know all of this?" I asked anxiously.

"It's not rocket science," Mrs. Perez said. "Dogs have puppies all the time."

By the time Mona arrived with a bag containing several kinds of dog food, Mike was nursing her brood and dozing. "I love what you've done with your front door," Mona said.

"Does the name Bitsy Stout mean anything to you?" I said dully.

"Have you heard anything more from her henchman?" she asked.

I told her about the late-night phone call.

Mrs. Perez called me to the laundry room. "You're going to have to keep an eye on the runt of the litter and make sure he nurses like the others," she said, showing me how to guide the tiniest of the puppies to a nipple.

"I can come home during lunch," I said, "but other than that, I have appointments all day."

"I'll stay with them this morning and look in on them from time to time over the next few days," she offered. "You have cable TV, right?"

I tried not to think about what I was going to do with a female dog and five puppies, as I greeted my first appointment of the day, a husband and wife who had decided to separate and were using me as a mediator. My first impulse had been to convince them to try to salvage their marriage, but their decision to divorce was a done deal.

To their credit, they were trying very hard to keep things amicable for the sake of their two children, whom I was also seeing separately. Although everybody seemed to be handling the situation well, it was still sad to witness the dissolution of a family.

Jay's family had not made me feel less loved after I'd left their son. Jay's father had worked at the same fire station and on the same shift as my dad. He had been there the night my father had not made it out of a burning building. While Jay's parents and siblings were disappointed over the split, they seemed to understand.

George Moss showed up at ten a.m. He did not look

happy, but at least he wasn't shoving vials in my face and threatening to blow up my office. I took that as a good sign, but I was cool to him as I invited him to sit down on my sofa.

"I know you're mad at me," George said, "but I was upset last time, on account of my wife leaving me."

I was silent.

"I'm sorry I did what I did," he said. He wiped his hand across his face. "I just have all this crap going on in my life. It's not fair."

I had to force myself not to overreact. If only he knew what was going on in *my* life. "What makes you think other people don't have crap going on?" I said. This was not the first time I'd asked him that question.

"See how you are?" he accused. "My life is in the shit house, and you're scolding me!"

"You know what, George?" I said. "I did you a favor by not having you arrested."

He glared at me. "I thought you were supposed to be my compassionate friend."

I didn't want to be George's friend. I realized I didn't even like George. I was tired of his drama and hysterics. I didn't blame his wife for leaving him. Bad enough she had to put up with that bony chest.

"Having a bad day does not give you the right to yell at or bully people," I said. "It's nobody's fault but yours that you choose to blow everything out of proportion."

"You're out of line, Doc," he said stiffly.

"I can't help you, Mr. Moss."

He sat up straighter on the sofa. "What the hell do you mean you can't help me? That's your job."

"I'll be glad to refer you to another therapist if you like, but that's the best I can do."

His face reddened and his eyes bulged. He was on the verge of God only knew what. I waited for him to whip out his vial.

"Then I demand that you give me all my money back," he shouted.

"We don't give refunds."

"We'll just see about that!"

There was a tap on the door. Mona peeked in. "Everything okay in here?" she asked.

George jumped to his feet. He looked at Mona as he pointed to me. "Your boss is a terrible therapist!" he yelled. "She is the worst therapist I've ever met."

Mona feigned a look of sheer horror. "That explains why nobody ever gets better!"

George flounced from my office and out of the reception room. "I'm in the wrong business," I told Mona.

"Don't talk like that," she said. "Even Dr. Phil has bad days."

I chuckled. "Face it, Mona. I'm never going to have my own TV show."

At lunch I drove home to check on Mike and the puppies. I was annoyed to find that Bitsy had still not washed the paint off, but I didn't have time to worry about it.

Mrs. Perez had left a note, promising to check back at three o'clock. I looked in the laundry room. Mom and kids were doing well, and Mike looked eager to see me. I let her out the back door so she could do her business.

"I need to make a doctor's appointment for you and your little ones, to make sure you're all okay," I said, once I let her in. "And we have to get you on birth control, because you've definitely exceeded your two-point-two limit." She wagged her tail as I thumbed through the Yellow Pages for a veterinarian in my area.

I dialed the number and explained my situation to the woman on the other end of the line. I was offered an appointment for eleven a.m. on Friday. I checked my purse-sized appointment book, saw that I was free, and promised to be there.

Mike returned to her box. Her children had caught on fast; they'd quickly discovered how to reach the milk supply. Well, all but one had, I noticed. The runt was having a hard time latching on to a nipple. Bad enough his eyes and ears were sealed closed; he had to try to squeeze between his larger brothers and sisters. I very gently aided him as Mrs. Perez had taught me, and I carried a chair inside so that I could sit and watch him. Once or twice he seemed to lose interest, but each time I led him back to a nipple and made sure he took in his mother's milk.

My last appointment of the day was with a nine-year-old boy with ADHD. He'd spent a portion of the previous school year serving in-school suspension, driving his parents crazy, and terrorizing the family cat until the poor animal began losing its hair. His parents and I, along with his teacher, had worked closely together, and we'd seen a lot of progress. The cat's hair had grown back.

Thad called as I was preparing to leave for the day.

"I'm ten minutes from your office. Can you meet me for a quick drink?" He paused. "It's urgent."

"What's wrong?" I asked.

"I'd prefer discussing it in person."

Thad sounded on the level. It didn't sound like he was going to ply me with wine before dangling a room key to the nearest hotel in my face. I thought of Mike, but I knew Mrs. Perez would have let her out several times.

"There's a new place not far from my office," I said. "It's called the Bistro." I gave him directions.

I stepped inside the restaurant fifteen minutes later and spotted Thad at one of the tables in the back. It would have been impossible to miss him, what with his thick blond hair and silk Italian suit. He was tanned, toned, and handsome. Thad had the sort of slick good looks you find in fashion advertisements, while Jay was the type you'd expect to find in an outdoors magazine.

Thad stood and pulled out my chair as I approached the table. I saw that he'd already ordered a glass of white wine for me.

I waited until we were both seated and I'd taken a sip

of wine. "What did you want to talk to me about?" I asked.

"It's really embarrassing," he said. "It's about Thomas. He's having serious marital problems; in fact, he and his wife have separated."

"I'm sorry to hear that," I said. I knew very little about Thad's younger brother, Thomas, having only seen him a couple of times at family functions. He did not resemble the blond and polished Glazers; his hair was dark and hung past his shoulders in a ponytail. Instead of attending an Ivy League college as was expected of him, he'd bought a feed-and-seed store far north of the city. I had not met Thomas's wife, a woman who was some years older and owned a small pig farm.

"The whole thing has gotten really nasty," Thad said. "I'd like for you to talk to Thomas before it escalates into something worse."

I held up my hand. "Wait. You're asking me to become involved in your family problems? No, thank you."

"Thomas likes you, Kate."

"He barely knows me!"

"Okay, the truth is, he likes you better than he likes his family. He'll listen to you. All I'm asking is that you calm him down before he goes off the deep end and does something he'll regret. Something we'll *all* regret," Thad added.

"Why would he go off the deep end?" I asked.

"I'd rather let him tell you," Thad said.

"Why me?"

"Because I know you'll keep it hush-hush. It wouldn't look so good for the family if it got out."

"Oh, so this is really about saving all of you from humiliation and has little to do with Thomas."

"Right." Thad nodded, then frowned. "Well, we *do* care what happens to him."

"I know I'm going to regret this."

Mike looked happy to see me when I arrived home; but, then, I was carrying a bag of fast food, so I wasn't certain whether it was the smell of fries sending her tail into a frantic wag or whether she had missed me. I let her out, checked the puppies, and replenished her food and water. I tried not to feel guilty as I stuffed my body with junk that was sure to clog my arteries.

After she ate, we went for a short walk, but I could tell by the time we turned back for the house that she was anxious to get back to her babies. Bitsy Stout was watering the plants on her porch and didn't see my approach. She gave a startled look when she glanced up and saw me standing on the sidewalk in front of her house.

"We need to talk about my front door," I said.

"You can't prove it was me," Bitsy said, and hurried inside her house before I could respond.

When I stepped through my front door with Mike, I noticed I had phone messages. Again, Jay had called and asked me to call him back. Just hearing his voice sent a shiver up my spine and filled my head with X-rated pictures.

I tried to push him from my mind. If I thought of him, I'd have to think about the upcoming divorce, and then I would have to wonder if I was making the biggest mistake of my life. On the other hand, I was almost certain that agreeing to see Thad's brother would top even that.

I could go round and round asking myself "what if" where my marriage was concerned, and it would get me exactly nowhere. Better to practice my multiplication tables.

There were a couple of hang-up calls, both accompanied by heavy breathing. I looked at my caller ID, but it read "unavailable."

I checked on Mike and the puppies and, as before, guided the runt to a nipple and sat in the chair while he nursed.

Thad's brother called me the next morning, only minutes after I arrived at the office. I hadn't yet poured a cup of coffee or checked the number of pens in the mug on my desk.

"I can see you at ten a.m.," I said, "if you can be here by then."

"I'll be there," he said.

He showed up as promised, looking as though he

hadn't slept in days. He wore jeans and a wrinkled T-shirt, he was unshaven, and his ponytail had grown considerably since I'd seen him. Mona looked perplexed as I led him inside my office.

"It's good to see you again, Thomas," I said, motioning for him to sit down. "I was sorry to hear that you're going through a hard time."

"I should never have married Lucille," he said, "but she seemed so nice when we met. And she was pretty, despite being quite a bit older than me." He sighed. "She was an exceptional pig farmer, too."

"What happened?"

"She started going through menopause. Got mean as hell. Got to where she'd jump down my throat every time I opened my mouth. I had no one to talk to but Homer."

"Who is Homer?"

"My pet hog. He was so small and straggly when he was born that Lucille said he was worthless. But he was such a cute little fellow that I insisted on keeping him around. Followed me like a puppy. I took him to town with me until he got too big to lift. Finally I told Homer I couldn't live with Lucille anymore, and I left."

I simply nodded.

Thomas continued. "She filed for a divorce. I got an apartment and started going out. I met someone I really liked. Then, a couple of nights ago, Lucille calls and says she went to the doctor, and she's feeling better. She tells me she wants to be friends, and she invites me to dinner. So I go to dinner, and she has cooked a big ham with all the fixings."

I could see his eyes watering. He looked embarrassed as he swiped them away. I could feel myself frowning. I had a sudden thought. "Is this going where I think it's going?" I asked, unable to believe it.

Tears slipped down his cheek. "It was Homer. Lucille didn't tell me until I'd eaten two hefty servings. She said it was payback for going out with a younger woman."

I was too stunned to speak. If Thomas hadn't looked so upset, I would have suspected Thad was playing a practical joke on me. "I'm sorry, Thomas," I finally said.

"I'll tell you, a woman going through menopause can be a dangerous thing," he said.

We just looked at each other for a moment. "How can I help?" I asked.

"My family and I are at odds right now. I want to have Lucille arrested for killing my hog. I want to sue her for all the emotional distress I've suffered. But my family, including Thad, is against it."

"Why?"

"They're afraid word will get out that a relative of theirs ate his pet hog. They have this great fear that some reporter will get his hands on the story, and that we'll all become laughingstocks." He frowned. "They want it swept under the rug, so to speak. You know what snobs my family can be."

Thomas was right; he did come from a long line of

snooty family. Thad could be a class-A snob when it suited him. "You have to decide what's best for you, Thomas," I said. "But I don't think you should do anything while you're this upset. I'd advise you to take a cooling-off period. Litigation can be costly, and it can drag on forever. How long do you want to stay caught up in all this pain and anger?"

He looked thoughtful. "It would probably jeopardize my new relationship. I don't want that to happen, on account of I need someone to talk to now that Homer is gone."

I just looked at him. I couldn't believe Thad had dragged me into this. I gave a reassuring smile. "Well, if you want my opinion, strictly as a friend, mind you," I said, "I think this is a perfect time to reach out to your big brother. I think Thad would be deeply hurt if you didn't turn to him in your time of need."

I left my office at the end of the day and drove to Wal-Mart. Inside, I headed for the pet section and selected a gentle dog shampoo for Mike that would not pose a threat to her nursing puppies. I searched through dog collars and leashes and, with a grin, chose a matching pink set with rhinestones. I grabbed another bag of dog food and a food-and-water dish labeled "Diva." It wasn't until I found myself looking at doggie raincoats that I suspected I might be going overboard.

As a kid, I'd never been allowed to have a dog. My

mother hated dogs because she claimed she'd come close to being mauled to death by one. Aunt Trixie had told me in confidence that the dog in question had been a poodle, and the bite had not broken the skin.

My mother was almost as bad as George Moss when it came to creating drama.

I was pulling out of the parking lot when I realized I was less than fifteen minutes from Jay's loft. I couldn't resist driving by. I was within a block of his place when I paused at a four-way stop. Behind me, a horn tooted. I groaned, recognizing Jay's SUV immediately. He climbed out and hurried toward my Toyota.

I rolled down my window, and he put his elbows on it and gave me that toe-curling smile. "Did you decide to come back home?" he asked. He wore a black T-shirt and snug faded jeans. He was toned and finely muscled and sexy as hell.

"Actually I was trying to avoid traffic." I could tell he wasn't buying it.

"How come you haven't returned my calls?"

I tried to avoid looking into those blue eyes. I could get lost in them and never find my way out. "I've been really busy, and I have all these obligations," I said quickly. "I have a new dog, and—"

"I thought dogs were forbidden in your family after your mother almost died from being attacked by a rabid Doberman."

"This dog followed me home, and then she had puppies."

"Wow." A horn blew. Jay motioned him around. "What are we going to do, Katie?" he said, fixing his gaze on me once more.

"This is not a good time for me, Jay."

"Perhaps you can work me in. Should I take a number?"

I put my car into park and gave a heated sigh. "Why do you want to talk *now*?" I demanded. "It has been almost six months. Six months," I repeated.

"Are we supposed to forget that Sunday night ever happened?"

"Oh, this is about sex."

"Not entirely."

Another horn blew. I glanced in my rearview mirror and saw half a dozen cars waiting. Again, Jay motioned them around. "Our circumstances haven't changed," I said.

"So we're back to that. My job," he added.

"Hello?" I waved a hand in his face. "It has always been about your job." A guy drove around Jay and flashed his middle finger.

Jay ignored it. "Why do you just *assume* I'm going to end up dead like your old man?"

I didn't respond.

"Why don't we do this, Kate? Why don't we, for the sake of argument, suppose that I might be better-skilled at my job than your father was at his?"

"That's a crummy thing to say!" I blurted.

"Yeah, well, it's pretty crummy that my wife has no

confidence in my skills despite my years of training. The department wouldn't have made me captain if they didn't think I knew what I was doing."

"You could have died, Jay!"

"But I didn't. It was a freak accident. An investigation later proved the building was not structurally sound to begin with, or it would never have collapsed. The fire was not hot enough at that point. I know what the hell I'm doing, Katie."

I had the ball of one hand pressed against my forehead. "I don't *care* that the building wasn't sound. I don't *care* that it was a freak accident. It happened, okay? And it scared the hell out of me." I wasn't going to tell him that all my old fears had come rushing back at me like a huge tidal wave. I wasn't going to tell him about the nightmares that followed. He would only accuse me of being irrational, as he'd done in the past. We would argue, and in the end nothing would get solved.

"I'm sorry, Katie," he said. "I'm sorry you got so scared that day."

A giant lump sprang to my throat at the gentleness in his voice. I opened my mouth to speak, only to be interrupted when the driver behind me leaned on his horn. I stuck my head out the window, ready to spew a litany of four-letter words at him, but I bit them back when I saw there were children in the car.

"I need to go." I put my car into gear. "Where's your foot?"

He opened his mouth to say something, and then closed it. Finally he stepped back, and I drove on. Tears burned my eyes. Nothing had been settled.

Mike just stared at me as I held up her new collar. "What? You don't like it?"

She cocked her head to the side, and her tail thumped against the floor. "I haven't wanted to bring this up," I said, "but you stink. I think a nice hot bubble bath is just the thing you need. That and a new collar, and you'll feel like a million bucks."

I grabbed the shampoo and headed upstairs. Mike followed and waited while I ran water in the tub. I wondered if she would freak out when I put her in the water, but when I carefully lifted her and set her down in it, she seemed to take it in stride. She stood perfectly still as I shampooed her twice. I wondered how a likeable, well-behaved dog had ended up a stray.

I towel-dried her, then used my blow-dryer on her wiry coat. I didn't want her damp when she rejoined her puppies. Last, I put the collar on her. "You're such a good girl," I said. "I have no doubt I'll be able to find a good home for you, as well as your puppies, when the time comes."

She fixed her big brown eyes on mine. "Don't look at me like that," I said. "I can't keep you. My life is too screwed up right now. *I'm* too screwed up. The fact that

I'm telling a dog all my problems should be a clear indication."

Mike waited while I cleaned the tub. I didn't know whether she was trying to be polite or whether some instinct told her I was about to go off the deep end. Since she did not seem in a hurry to rejoin the puppies, I took her for a brief walk, using her new leash. Afterward I sat by the box in the laundry room and saw that the runt nursed. In the kitchen, I tried to decide what to cook for dinner. It was already getting late. Finally I pulled some tuna fish from my cabinet, drained it, and ate it right out of the can as Mike watched.

"See what I mean?" I said. "This is no way to live."

The phone rang. Thad spoke from the other end and wasted no time getting to the point. "Did you talk Thomas out of going to an attorney?"

"I can't discuss what went on in a private session," I said.

"It wasn't a real session. You just talked to him."

"Why don't *you* talk to him, Thad? It wouldn't kill you to get involved in your brother's life."

"We have nothing in common. Thomas is in a bowling league, for Pete's sake!"

"Oh, like I have anything in common with *my* family, better known as Dysfunctional 'R' Us?"

"Let's face it, Kate; you're a better woman than I am a man."

"You're not as shallow and insensitive as you pretend

to be. I know that deep down you're a decent human being."

Thad sighed. "I hate it when you try to make me into something I'm not."

"I believe in you, Thad."

"It would be so much easier to just buy Thomas another hog," he said before he hung up.

chapter 7

· ·

Mona and I sipped coffee in the kitchen before Nancy and my first patient of the day arrived. I noticed that Mona looked worried.

"I'm thinking this thing with Liam and me isn't going to work out," she said. "He's tired all the time. He has problems holding his eyes open at dinner. I think that's the only reason he hasn't pushed for sex; he doesn't have the energy. Of course, there's always the possibility that he's not really attracted to me."

"He certainly seemed attracted when he came by to pick you up for dinner," I said, "but I know medical school is a bear."

"Exactly," she said with a nod. "I need a man who has more time to devote to *me*." She took a sip of her coffee. "But enough about me. Why do *you* look worried?"

"I'm concerned about one of Mike's puppies," I said. "The runt," I added.

"When do you see the vet?" she asked.

"Friday was the earliest appointment I could get." I gave a wide yawn. I'd gotten up several times during the night to make sure the runt ate.

"Don't let it stress you," Mona said. "You and Mrs. Perez are doing a great job." She paused. "Anything else on your mind?" she asked.

There were times when I felt Mona could read my thoughts. I shrugged. "I guess I'm having a case of pre-divorce jitters."

"It's not too late to change your mind, you know."

"It's complicated."

"So you've said. But complicated and irreparable aren't the same."

I was thankful that Nancy chose that moment to come through the door. I couldn't explain my feelings to Mona when I didn't understand them myself.

I was dragging by late afternoon. Bad enough I'd lost so much sleep the night before; the morning had not gone well. One of my clinically depressed patients had taken a nosedive after discovering her husband's infidelity. Later, a family counseling session that included a troubled teen had turned into a yelling match between father and son.

I felt confident that I had helped in each case, but it

had taken the wind out of me. To make matters worse, Mona was down in the dumps at the thought of breaking it off with Liam, and Nancy feared she would never find a job. I also feared Nancy would not find a job before I got caught with a nail salon in my kitchen.

All in all, I could not wait for the day to end. I was counting the hours until I could climb into my bed and put the day behind me. I splashed cold water on my face, gulped back a cup of strong coffee, and waited for my last patient of the day to arrive.

Arnie Decker was a forty-seven-year-old ex-Marine who'd served in the Persian Gulf. I'd treated a number of military personnel for posttraumatic stress disorder; I recognized the signs well since PTSD had been the topic of my dissertation. But Arnie did not suffer from it.

He was simply lonely. He was the loneliest person I knew. Two failed marriages and a slew of relationships that had gone nowhere had convinced Arnie he was better off alone. Which was sad, because he was a strapping blond-going-gray who, thanks to Uncle Sam, had learned the importance of good physical fitness and sharply creased slacks.

A month's worth of sessions had gotten us nowhere; my gentle prodding to get Arnie to open up had made him more tight-lipped than ever. So we discussed his job as a chef in a four-star French restaurant, and I was privy to the secret ingredients that made his elaborate dishes the talk of the town. That Arnie would share those ingredients proved he trusted me. That he could not bring himself to give me the exact measurements showed we still had a way to go.

Arnie was in the process of listing the ingredients of his new and improved béarnaise sauce when I found my thoughts drifting and my yawns harder to hide. My eyes burned, and my lashes felt as though tiny weights had been attached to them. I did not realize I'd dozed off until Arnie suddenly cried out in indignation, jolting me from my mininap.

"I can't believe you fell asleep on me!" he said. "There are chefs in town who would kill for this recipe."

To say I was mortified was an understatement. I straightened in my chair, an apology on my tongue. Instead I crossed my arms and gazed coolly at him.

"You know what, Arnie? Next to me, you have the most boring life in the world. I don't know *why* you're here, but I don't think it's to bounce recipe ideas off me. Until you decide to open up and tell me what's *really* bugging you, you're wasting your time and money coming here."

I had to pause to catch my breath.

Arnie just stared. Then he hung his head. "You're right, Dr. Kate."

I didn't know what to say, but I tried not to act surprised that I might have accidentally touched on something.

"The truth is, I'm so damn lonely I don't know what to do. I can't have a successful marriage, and I don't fit in with my old Marine buddies. I don't fit in anywhere.

126

I'm an outcast. I'm in pain, but I'm too embarrassed to talk about my problem."

I softened at the look in Arnie's eyes. He really was in pain, so much that I could almost forgive him for being boring. My first thought was that Arnie was gay. It would explain the failed marriages and relationships and why he didn't fit in with the guys.

"Okay, so you're gay," I said.

He shook his head.

"Bisexual?"

"Nope."

"Cross-dresser?"

Another shake of the head.

"Then what?"

He covered his eyes. "This is so hard."

"Come on, Arnie. It's not my job to judge my clients." He refused to look at me. "Don't make me arm wrestle the information out of you," I said, trying to put him at ease.

Finally he dragged his hands down his face and met my eyes. "Dr. Kate, you're looking at a woman trapped in a man's body."

I'll admit I hadn't seen it coming. "Okay!" I said, trying to sound as though I dealt with that sort of thing all the time so I would lessen his shame. "You simply have a transgender issue," I said. "It's more prevalent than you think." Actually, I couldn't recall the statistics; there were more gender and sexual orientation disorders than Mona had credit cards. It didn't help that one disorder could be mistaken for or overlap another. "It'll take some time and work, but we can deal with it. Together," I added.

"I know all about gender identity disorders," he said dully. "I've researched them. Do you have any idea what it's like for me to walk around acting all macho and praying nobody finds out my toenails are painted?" As if acting on impulse, he suddenly pulled off one shoe and sock, and stuck out his foot so that I could see his red toenails.

I shook my head sadly. "Oh, Arnie."

"I knew you'd be disgusted."

"Who wouldn't be," I said. "That's the worst nail-painting I've ever seen."

He put down his foot, clearly offended. "So I'm not an expert. You don't have to be rude."

"Trust me, I'm telling you for your own good." I checked my wristwatch. "Look, we're out of time, but we have made a lot of headway today. In the meantime, why don't you let me schedule you an appointment with our manicurist in the back? Believe me, a good pedicure will go a long way toward making you feel better."

I arrived home to find my front door splattered with dried egg. The broken shells beneath it suggested that an entire dozen had been used as artillery. I was stunned. Had Bitsy lost her mind? Or had one of her nutcase church members decided to join her in making my life miserable?

I muttered a four-letter word and marched across the street. I banged on Bitsy Stout's door a full five minutes before she finally answered.

"Are you crazy?" I shouted. "You can't just go around defacing other people's property."

Bitsy hitched her jaw in defiance. "You can't prove I did it."

"I don't need proof. You're the only nutso neighbor I've got, and if you set foot on my property again, you're going to regret it."

"Are you threatening me?"

"Call it what you like, but if I catch you in my yard again, I'll sic my dog on you."

Bitsy smirked. "That little thing couldn't hurt a housefly."

I hate smirks. I wanted to smack that smirk right off of her face. Instead I crossed my arms and smirked right back at her. "Well, for your information, her father was a pit bull and dangerously vicious."

Bitsy slammed the door in my face. I crossed the street, went inside my house, and let Mike out to relieve herself. By the time she returned, I'd changed into jeans and a T-shirt and taken a couple of pictures of the crime scene. I had no idea how I was going to build a case against Bitsy, but I couldn't afford to let her damage my door so severely that I was forced to replace it.

I filled a bucket with hot sudsy water. I scrubbed and muttered foul words for more than an hour and was rinsing away the soap with a garden hose when the police pulled up.

I watched the officers cross my yard. "Are you Kate Holly?" the older one asked.

I immediately became anxious. Had something happened to Jay? Had my mother and aunt been in an accident? "Yes," I said quickly. "What's wrong?"

"We got a call from one of your neighbors that you threatened her life."

I gave a huge sigh. "I don't believe this."

"Did you or did you not threaten to unleash your killer attack dog on your neighbor Miss Stout?"

I tried to think my way out of getting arrested, but before I could answer, a familiar black SUV pulled up. Jay climbed out and crossed the yard.

"Good afternoon, officers," he said politely. "I understand we have a little problem here."

"Who are you?" the younger officer asked.

"I know who he is," the other man said, regarding Jay. They shook hands. "Who called the fire department?"

"Nobody," Jay said. "I heard it over the scanner. Figured you guys might need backup. This is one dangerous woman you're dealing with. I'm married to her, so I should know."

I was sure Bitsy Stout was peering out her window at the whole thing. "That's really funny, Jay," I said.

"Your wife supposedly threatened to sic her attack dog on an old lady."

"She also made lewd and lascivious gestures," the younger one said.

Jay looked at me. "Dang, Kate. That's no way to treat a senior citizen."

I tried to explain my side of the story. "It started with that sculpture," I said, pointing to it. "Bitsy calls it pornographic."

All three men studied it closely. "What's it supposed to be?" the younger one asked.

"It's called *First Man and Woman*. I think it's supposed to be Adam and Eve in the Garden of Eden."

"I'll bet I know where you got that," Jay said, looking amused.

"What's that thing there?" the younger cop asked, pointing to the man.

I gave an enormous sigh. "A leaf."

Jay continued to look amused as I told them how Bitsy had defaced my door twice. His smile faded when I told them about the threatening phone call at work.

"Did you file a complaint?" the older officer asked, still studying the statue.

"No. I'm sort of in the process of building my case."

"Well, we need to get a look at the animal," he said.

I opened the door and stepped back so they could enter. I led them to my utility room. As if acting on cue, Mike was lying in her box, looking docile, while her puppies nursed. She wagged her tail.

"That's your killer attack dog?" the younger officer said.

"Yep," I said as Mike's tail thumped against the cardboard box. "She is just disguised as a puny little mutt who recently gave birth."

The young cop grinned. "Hey, those are some cute puppies. My kids would love to have a puppy."

"It can be arranged," I assured him.

The older cop shook his head. "Look, you can get into a lot of trouble by threatening people," he said. "Especially old ladies," he added. "I'm going to give you a warning this time, but if it happens again, you're not going to be so lucky."

I opened my mouth to protest, but Jay cut me off. "Nod your head, Katie," he said. "Promise the policeman you'll play nice from now on. You do *not* want to go to jail. Bad things can happen to good girls who land in jail."

I gulped and nodded fiercely.

"See that?" Jay said to the men. "She's learned her lesson."

"Okay, we're done here," the older cop said to his partner, who handed me his card and asked me to call him when I was ready to find homes for the puppies. I escorted them to the door, still nodding.

"That was a close call," Jay said once I'd closed the door. "I could use a cold beer. I think I deserve it for getting your butt out of a sling. And then I want to hear about the guy who called and threatened you."

I was too shaken to speak. I remembered I had exactly

one beer in my refrigerator. Jay followed me to the kitchen, and I pulled it out. He opened it. Instead of taking a drink, he handed it to me. I took a long swig.

"Well?" he asked.

I handed him the beer and repeated what I'd said only minutes before.

"What makes you so sure it has something to do with Bitsy whatever-her-last-name-is?"

"It makes sense that her church group would rally around her, since they all think I'm displaying pornography." I sighed. "I wish I'd never seen that statue."

"You think I need to hang out here for a few days just in case this guy shows up?"

"No. I'm hoping the whole thing will blow over."

"I want you to keep me posted."

We took turns sipping the beer. My stomach growled. Jay smiled. "How about we grab dinner?"

"I don't know if that's wise," I said. "We're getting divorced Friday of next week."

"But this is Thursday of *this* week."

We went back and forth for several minutes before I finally gave in. I can be so weak at times. All I have to do is look into those blue eyes, and I'm a goner.

"I'll agree to go this *one time*, okay? But I'm paying my own way, because I don't want you to get the wrong idea."

"The wrong idea?" he asked quizzically.

"Yeah. Like you can just waltz back into my life and expect to pick up where we left off."

He pretended to be shocked. "I would never think that, Katie. I've come to terms with the fact that we no longer find each other irresistible."

I knew he was lying. He knew I knew he was lying. But I was hungry, and the thought of eating canned tuna was even scarier than sitting across a table from my soon-to-be-ex-husband and trying hard not to get caught up in his good looks or in those smiles that made my nerve endings do happy dances.

"Okay," I said. "As long as we understand each other."

We headed for the door. Jay paused to open it for me. "And just to make you feel better, let me say that I almost never think about sex with you."

chapter 8

....

"*You did not* tell me we were going to Rusty's Place," I said when it was apparent Jay was headed in that direction.

"What's wrong with Rusty's Place? It used to be your favorite."

Which is why I didn't want to go there, I wanted to tell him. I had stayed away from Rusty's after separating from Jay. It had been *our* place. The jukebox had *our* songs. Jay and I had a favorite table. "Okay," I said, figuring I may as well get it over with. Jay and I had history. I couldn't avoid every place we'd ever been together.

I didn't miss the shocked looks we received from Rusty or his waitresses when we stepped through the front door ten minutes later. Rusty personally met us with menus. He gave me a hug and made the usual small talk. I noticed he hadn't lost the belly that suggested he liked the food he served.

"Does this mean you two are getting back together?" he asked.

I tugged playfully at his short beard. "It means we got hungry at the same time."

He started to lead us to our old table. "Could we sit by the window instead?" I asked. Jay looked amused. Rusty shrugged and led us to it.

"Drinks are on the house," he announced.

Jay and I ordered drafts and New York strips. "I see nothing has changed," I said once we were alone. Same dark paneling on the walls, the same customers at the long bar, which offered discounted appetizers and booze at happy hour. I wondered whether Jay had brought dates there.

"I think Rusty is more concerned with serving good food than making cosmetic changes," Jay said, "but that's what I like about the place. You want some quarters for the jukebox?"

I shook my head. "I'm not really in the mood for music."

He grinned. "What *are* you in the mood for?"

"A nice thick steak cooked just the way I like it."

"Then you're in the right place." Jay took a sip of his beer and leaned back in his chair. "How is the practice coming along?" he asked.

"I'm getting new patients here and there," I told him.

"Anybody interesting?"

I'd always felt comfortable discussing my patients with Jay, although I never mentioned names. "I had someone threatening to blow up my office with fake nitroglycerin."

He immediately frowned. "What makes you think it's fake?"

I told him about the vial of insulin George Moss was forced to keep with him for his diabetes. "This patient is histrionic, a male version of a drama queen. If he doesn't get his way, he throws temper tantrums and threatens people."

"It bothers me that you're not taking him seriously," Jay said. "You only have to watch the news to see what people are capable of making right in their own kitchens. You should let me ask a friend from the APD to look into it, Katie."

"He's not my patient anymore," I said. "I called Thad and told him to find the guy another therapist."

I noted the sudden stiffening of Jay's jaw. He'd never liked Thad, but it was easy to figure out why.

"Just be careful," Jay said.

I didn't know if he was warning me about George Moss, or Thad, or both.

"Wait till you get a load of the new chiropractor on the sixth floor, who just happens to be single," Mona said when I walked into the office the next morning. "He's hot."

"Does this mean you're going to stop seeing Liam?" I asked.

Her eyes clouded. "I should probably back off slowly and just be friends with him. Think what it would be like to fall in love with somebody like Liam. I mean, the man is gorgeous, and I haven't even seen him naked yet."

"Okay, so he's gorgeous. What's the problem?"

"Maybe he's too gorgeous. Plus, he's surrounded by all those sweet young things at school."

"Yeah, but he seems to prefer you," I pointed out.

"For now," she said. "But he's young. How do I know he'll feel that way in ten years when I'm forty-three? Botox injections can only do so much, you know."

She looked away, and I got the impression she didn't want to talk about it. "So when are you going out with this hot new chiropractor?" I asked, changing the subject.

"We haven't actually met yet. I'm planning my strategy. I'm sure the competition will be stiff. Every woman in the building is going to be after him."

"I'm really confused. How is that different from what you just described with Liam?"

"Dr. Manning—that's his name—is closer to my age. I wouldn't be self-conscious getting naked with him."

"Oh, well. When you say it like that, it makes perfect sense." I headed toward the kitchen for a cup of coffee.

My first patient of the morning was Harold Fry, a manic depressive sent to me by none other than Thad

Glazer. When Harold took his medication and showed up for our weekly therapy sessions, he managed his life pretty well. When Harold got off his medication—he hated the side effects—he became Agent Fry, CIA operative, working in espionage.

One look at Harold in his beige trench coat, hat, and sunglasses, and I knew he had probably flushed his lithium tablets down the toilet again.

Mona was intrigued by Harold. He did not appear delusional when he discussed (in strict confidence, mind you) his past and present assignments with the CIA. Although it would have been unethical for me to tell Mona that Harold was bipolar and borrowing his tales from his late grandfather, who'd authored dozens of spy novels, I had warned her not to take him seriously.

Inside my office, Harold spent the first ten minutes checking to see whether the room or my phone was bugged. When he was convinced it was safe to speak, he leaned forward on the sofa and motioned me closer.

"There is a new tenant in my building," he said. "His name is Vladimir Guchkov. I saw it with my own eyes, listed on his mailbox. He's a professor. He plans to teach Russian history at the university."

"That has you concerned?" I asked.

Harold nodded. "I've done some checking. You'd be surprised how many Russian professors there are in this country. There are even a couple at Harvard. It's clear they're infiltrating our colleges and brainwashing our students into becoming Communist sympathizers."

"And you feel confident you can put a stop to it?"

Harold sat up straight and squared his shoulders. "Absolutely," he said. "This is my area of expertise, after all."

Harold's so-called expertise, his feelings of specialness, that only he could save the world from Russian invasion, were a clear case of grandiosity and a dead giveaway that he was in full-blown mania. He would work tirelessly and spend great amounts of money, if need be, to prove his claims. Those delusions of grandeur were what set Harold apart from the paranoid schizophrenics, even though I personally felt he suffered from paranoia. Thad and I were not in full agreement about that.

"Have you discussed your suspicions with Dr. Glazer?" I asked, knowing that Thad saw Harold once a month for medication checks.

"I don't trust Dr. Glazer," Harold said. "I think he's trying to erase my memory. Why else would he send me to those laboratories where people in white coats are always sticking needles in me and taking my blood?"

"Dr. Glazer is not trying to erase your memory, Harold," I said, having had this conversation with him before. "He is checking your lithium levels."

"So he says."

"I think we need to give Dr. Glazer a call," I said.

Harold didn't look pleased. "Okay, but can I use your bathroom first?"

"Sure." It would give me a chance to speak to Thad

privately about Harold. I picked up the phone and dialed Thad's office as Harold left the room. His receptionist informed me that he had taken the day off to go fishing with his brother. I was impressed that Thad had decided to reach out to Thomas, but I still needed to talk to him about Harold. I left a message for him to call me as soon as possible.

I knew that Thad would want to admit Harold to the psych ward until he was safely on his meds, but Harold hated hospitals. Fortunately Harold had a sister in town, and she had helped get him back on track once before. I felt certain we could enlist her again.

I waited for Harold to return. When he didn't, I stepped outside my office. I found Mona at her desk looking through a Tiffany catalog. "Where is Harold?" I asked.

"He said he had to be somewhere."

"Oh, great!" I muttered and raced from the reception area. I should have known Harold would bolt at the sound of Thad's name.

I caught the elevator just as the door was about to close. I got off on the main floor and hurried outside, but there was no sign of Harold. I cased the parking lot, peeking through car windows. It had started to rain. The sky was dark, clouds rolling in. Finally I gave up.

Mr. Lewey was sitting in the reception room when I returned. I did my best to act calm and natural, knowing Mr. Lewey would immediately pick up on my anxiety and go into panic mode. "Do me a favor," I said to

Mona. "In about half an hour, start calling Mr. Fry's home number. Tell him he needs to come back in and see me."

"I'm on it," she said and went back to her catalog.

I ushered Mr. Lewey inside my office and closed the door.

"Today is the day," he said.

His announcement was followed by a roll of thunder. I glanced out my window and saw a flash of lightning in the distance. The rain was coming down hard. I turned back to him. "The day for what?" I asked.

"I'm ready to get on the elevator. Today. Now."

I couldn't hide my surprise. "What brought about the sudden change?" I asked.

"I just made up my mind to do it, even if it kills me."

I could see his fists balled at his side, his teeth gritted. "You look like you're ready to go into battle," I said. I'd barely gotten the words out before a loud clap of thunder rattled the windows in my office and made him jump. "I don't want you to fight the fear, Mr. Lewey. We've discussed how that only makes it worse."

"I don't care *how* I have to do it," he said. "I just want to get it over with. You're either with me or you're not."

I followed a determined Mr. Lewey from my office. Mona was dialing a number on the phone. "Mr. Lewey and I need to step out for a moment."

Mona nodded and gave Mr. Lewey the thumbs-up sign. He'd obviously told her of his decision.

Mr. Lewey and I were both doing deep-breathing

exercises as we waited for the elevator. No doubt he was trying to remain calm now that he'd made a decision to conquer his fear. I, on the other hand, was trying to figure out what to do about Harold Fry's disappearance. I worried he would never set foot in my office again if I participated in having him hospitalized. Any progress we'd made trying to control his mood swings and manic episodes would go down the toilet.

The elevator doors opened. Fortunately it was empty. Mr. Lewey and I stepped inside; he went to the back. I held the door open with my foot. "How are you?"

He took a shaky breath. "I'm about a seven or eight, but I'm okay. Let's take it to the top."

I stepped back, and the metal doors closed. I punched the tenth-floor button, and we started up. I turned to Mr. Lewey and found him plastered against the back of the elevator, white-knuckling the rail. His eyes were squinched closed. "Why don't you stand at the front beside me?" I said. "You can press the button and make it stop if you need to get off."

"I'm fine."

But he didn't look fine. Perspiration beaded his brow; his breathing was shallow. I feared he would hyperventilate. We reached the top floor, and the doors opened. "Let's get off here," I said, convinced the whole thing had been a bad idea.

"Keep going," he said between clenched teeth. The doors closed before I could stop them. The elevator paused on the eighth floor, and a woman got on bearing an umbrella. She shot a curious look at Mr. Lewey before turning to me.

"Some weather we're having," she said. "It's getting downright nasty outside. I hear we're under a severe thunderstorm warning."

"Be careful driving," I told her, even as I darted looks at Mr. Lewey.

We started down again. We'd almost reached the lobby floor when the lights flickered, followed by a boom of thunder that seemed to shake the entire building. The elevator gave a jolt and went completely black.

"Uh-oh!" Mr. Lewey said.

"Looks like we're stuck," the woman said.

"Uh-oh!" Mr. Lewey said more loudly.

"We're not stuck," I said in the darkness. "Just give it a second. The lights will come back on."

"No, no, this is really bad!" Mr. Lewey was clearly having a panic attack.

"What's *his* problem?" the woman asked.

Without warning, Mr. Lewey shoved me aside so hard I bumped my elbow on the rail. I could hear him gasping and struggling. "What are you doing?" I asked.

"Trying to pry open the door before our oxygen supply runs out!" he yelled. "We're all going to die!"

"Oh no!" the woman said. "I'm stuck in an elevator with a maniac." She began banging on the door as well. "Help!" she cried.

"Move out of my way, lady," Mr. Lewey ordered. "Where is that damn phone?"

"Don't touch me, you weirdo!"

I heard several thumps. Mr. Lewey yelped. "Stop hitting me with your umbrella, you old bag!"

"Both of you stop it!" I shouted as Mr. Lewey grappled for the phone and began shouting into it that we were all dying, even though we'd only been stopped little more than a minute.

"Mr. Lewey, I think we should practice our deep-breathing exercises," I said.

"How the hell are we going to do that when there is no air!" he yelled. "We're going to die in here. I'm passing out!"

I heard him hit the floor only a split second before the lights flashed on. The elevator gave a jolt and started down. The door opened, and the crowd waiting to get on stepped back as the woman with the umbrella cried out in alarm, "Let me out of here! That man is a psycho!"

Mr. Lewey scrambled to his feet, touched his face. "I'm alive! I'm alive!"

"Mr. Lewey, why don't we go back up to my office and—"

He wasn't listening. He all but hurled himself from the elevator, pushed through the small crowd, and exited via the double glass doors leading outside.

I ran after him, even as the rain pelted my face and lightning flashed ominously in the dark sky, even as I wondered whether other psychologists were forced to chase their patients through parking lots on a regular basis. Had I not been so caught up in my thoughts, I might have noticed the steel drainage grate in the asphalt parking lot. Which was why I was so surprised when the heel of my shoe jammed inside one of the holes. I immediately fell forward. I tried to catch my fall with my hands. Pain shot through my left wrist.

A car skidded toward me. I glanced up to see a panicked Mr. Lewey behind the wheel, headed straight toward me in an old, battered red Ford Mustang. I closed my eyes and prepared to die, just as he swerved to one side to keep from running over me. He hit a speed bump so hard that his tires left the pavement for a split second before landing hard in a mud puddle. Black, oily water sprayed my face and hair. His back hubcap flew off, came at me like a Frisbee, and bounced off my head. Then all went black.

chapter 9

·····························

When I opened my eyes I found myself lying just inside the lobby, on what appeared to be a blanket made up of men's jackets. Someone had covered me with another one. A sweet-smelling woman pressed ice to my head. I heard two men in the background arguing the merits of having moved me.

"You just opened yourself up to a lawsuit, pal," one of them said. "You're never supposed to move someone who has been badly injured."

"You're saying we should have left her in the parking lot, where she could have been struck by lightning?" the other man said. "What a jerk!"

"Please stop fussing!" the woman holding the ice to my head told them. "She's awake."

I blinked up at her. "How badly am I injured?" I asked.

"You have a bump on your forehead, hon. An ambulance is on the way. How's your vision?"

I vaguely recognized her. She wore a nurse's uniform. "I can see okay, but my wrist hurts," I told her.

"Try to lie very still," she said. "Is there someone we can call? A relative?" she added.

I had to think for a moment. I did not want to give my mother's name: I knew she would go ape on me. I debated telling the nurse I was an orphan.

Then I heard, "Eek. Oh, my God! Is she dead?"

I recognized Mona's voice. She pushed through the crowd and gave a huge gasp. "Kate, are you okay? What happened to you?"

"Mr. Lewey flipped out on the elevator and almost ran over me in the parking lot."

"We're waiting on the ambulance," the nurse said to Mona, even as I heard a siren in the distance. "You might want to try to contact a relative."

I looked at Mona. "Please don't call the Junk Sisters."

I arrived at the ER, where I was immediately placed on a gurney and wheeled into X-ray. When I was returned to my cubicle in the ER, I found Jay waiting.

"Mona said she was told to contact your next of kin," he said and grinned. "I knew you'd choose me."

"Where is Mona?"

"She's on her way. She figured she should cancel your appointments for the day. How're you feeling?"

148

"Not so good."

Jay was interrupted from answering when the staff surgeon, Dr. Beau Bodine, reappeared, carrying my X-rays. He had a shock of red hair and wore the usual green hospital garb. He looked surprised to see Jay. "Is the hospital on fire?"

Jay shook his head. "I hope not. I just finished a twenty-four-hour shift, and I'm not in the mood to work. Actually, I'm married to this pretty lady."

"No way!" Bodine said.

Jay looked at me. "Katie, you've probably heard me mention Bobo. He and I play racquetball at the gym a couple of times a week."

"Bobo is my nickname," Dr. Bodine told me.

"Tell her your other nickname."

Bobo's face turned as red as his hair. "This might not be the right time."

"They call him Knife," Jay said.

I gulped.

"I have good news and bad news," Bobo said to me. "The good news is, you don't have a concussion. That knot on your head should go down in a couple of days if you keep icing it. The bad news is, you've got one hell of a wrist fracture. We could set it and slap on a cast, but I'd have trouble sleeping at night if I didn't put in a couple of pins."

"Surgery?" I asked, giving another gulp.

" 'Fraid so. You won't have much of a scar, though. You'll still be able to wear a bikini."

"Yeah, but will she still be able to bear my children?" Jay asked.

"I wouldn't recommend it," Bobo said. "I have three kids, and my life is hell."

"Could you guys get serious for one minute here?" I said.

"I'm sorry," Bobo said.

"Will it hurt?" I asked.

"What, the surgery?" Bobo nodded. "Damn right it'll hurt. Which is why I was thinking I might knock you out first," he added. "It'll cost a little more, but I think it's worth it. Once you wake up, you can go home. You'll be groggy for a while: I plan to give you good drugs."

"What do I need to do?"

Bobo shrugged. "Just sign a couple of forms stating you won't sue me if I accidentally operate on the wrong wrist. Next thing you know, you'll be in la-la land."

Mona showed up while I was waiting for the forms. Jay had gone to get me a cup of water. "Everything is taken care of," she said. "I rescheduled your patients, and I spoke to Thad's secretary."

"Did you tell her Harold Fry was missing?"

"Yes. She promised to tell Thad as soon as he called in. Also, she assured me he wouldn't mind taking any emergency calls you might have." Mona sighed dramatically. "No telling what you're going to have to do in return for that little favor."

"I'll probably have to let him look up my dress," I said wearily. "What about Mike and the puppies?"

"Mrs. Perez is on it. How badly are you hurt?"

I filled her in. "I'm going to be operated on by a guy named Bobo the Knife. First, though, I have to sign a statement that I won't get mad at him if he screws up."

"Wow, that sounds pretty scary," Mona said. "They need to put you on a morphine drip. That way you won't care *what* happens."

When I opened my eyes, I found Mona and Jay standing beside my bed. "Welcome back," Jay said.

"Is it over?"

"Yes. And, look, you have a nice new cast on your wrist. Bobo insisted on signing it."

I wanted to go back to sleep.

"Jay has offered to take you home and stay with you," Mona said. "I made him promise there will be no messing around unless you are fully conscious."

Mona and a nurse helped me into my clothes. I drifted off several times as Jay drove me home. Mike met us at the front door.

"She might need to go out," I said.

Jay let her out the back, then joined me in the laundry room, where I was checking on her litter. "What are you going to do with all these puppies?" he asked.

"I don't know." I suddenly remembered I was supposed to take them to the vet that morning. I made a mental note to reschedule once I stopped feeling loopy.

Jay let Mike back in. I found a note on my kitchen

table from Mrs. Perez. She had taken care of my doggie-farm chores, straightened my house, and put clean sheets on my bed.

God bless Mrs. Perez.

Jay helped me upstairs to my bedroom. Mike followed and watched us closely. I looked at myself in the mirror and groaned. "I have to take a shower and wash my hair," I said.

"Great. We can shower together."

I gave him my sternest look.

"Maybe not," he said. "You'll need to keep that cast dry. Sit on the bed while I find something."

I sat on the bed. Mike came over and licked my hand as though she understood I wasn't feeling well.

It seemed like forever before Jay returned with his supplies. He wrapped a small plastic garbage bag around my wrist and fastened it on with rubber bands and tape. I grabbed clean underwear and my favorite long T-shirt, and stepped inside the bathroom.

"I'll be right outside," Jay said. "Be careful."

I showered and washed my hair in record time. The hot water felt great on my bruised and sore body. I emerged from the bathroom in my T-shirt, with wet hair.

"I'll bet you bought that at one of those sexy lingerie stores," he said.

"I didn't want to risk turning you on."

"You could send ice water through a man's loins in that thing. Are you hungry?" he asked.

"Maybe later," I said. My shower had tired me. I crawled beneath my covers and went to sleep. I was nudged awake later, and found Jay holding a food tray. He put it on my lap. Waffles. "Yum," I managed in a groggy voice. I winced as pain shot through my head.

"I figured they would hit the spot."

I didn't have to ask where he'd gotten them. Waffle House wasn't far. Jay knew that when I wasn't feeling well or was really tired, I often craved pancakes or waffles. "This is so nice of you," I said, digging in. I noticed it was almost eight p.m., which explained why I was as hungry as a bear.

"I filled your prescription for pain pills while I was out. You were due to take one a couple of hours ago." He uncapped the bottle and handed me one. I took it gratefully. "Has Mike been out?"

"Yeah. She's been worried about you. I put her on the bed beside you so she could sniff you and make sure you were okay. Mrs. Perez came by and showed me how to get the runt to eat, and Mona called to check on you."

"I'm sorry you had to spend the day babysitting me," I said. "I know you have things to do."

"Are you trying to get rid of me?"

"I don't like to impose."

"You're not imposing, Katie."

I averted my gaze. It was too tempting to fall back into the role of being Jay's wife. Being Jay's wife made me crazy. I spent a lot of time thinking about burning skyscrapers. Atlanta had a lot of skyscrapers compared to, say, Cowpens, South Carolina. I could handle being Jay's wife in a place like Cowpens.

Better to get my own waffles than to live in constant worry.

I finished eating, and Jay took the tray. I could feel the pain pill making me loose, and my headache wasn't so bad anymore. I lay back on the pillow and closed my eyes.

I heard a thunk on my nightstand and knew it was Jay setting a cup of coffee there for me. Funny how things stick with you. I opened my eyes. My headache was back, and my wrist hurt.

"Good morning," Jay said.

I sat up slowly. "I didn't mean for you to stay all night." I glanced at the pillow beside me and saw his head print.

He shrugged. "I'm off for forty-eight hours. How are you feeling?"

"A couple of aspirin wouldn't hurt. I can't afford to go into the office groggy."

"As your care provider, I wouldn't recommend going to work today."

"I have to. Some of my patients get edgy if they don't see me every week." I reached for my coffee cup and took a careful sip, and was reminded that Jay had a knack for making good java. "Could you give me a ride to the office?"

"If you're sure," he said. "I'll get your aspirin." He went into the bathroom.

I heard him open my medicine cabinet. I glanced at the alarm clock. Seven thirty. I was pretty sure it was Saturday. I tried to remember when my first patient was due in, but my appointment book was sitting on my desk at the office. I called Mona at home.

"Did you and Jay *do it*?" she asked first thing.

"Not that I recall."

"How're you feeling?"

Jay handed me two aspirin. "Better," I said. "Do you know what time my first patient is supposed to arrive?"

"I rearranged your schedule," she said. "You're free until ten. Also, you'll have a couple of hours down time at lunch in case you need to rest. Do you think you're up to it?"

"Yeah. I have to find Harold Fry and Mr. Lewey."

"I've already spoken to Mr. Lewey," Mona said, "and I let him have it for almost running over you."

"He wasn't really trying to run over me," I said. "He swerved in the nick of time."

"He's still a jerk. As for Harold Fry, I had no luck, but I'll keep trying." We hung up.

Jay looked at me. "A patient tried to run over you yesterday?" he said in disbelief. He didn't wait for a response. "Another patient is threatening to blow up your office with nitroglycerin? And you're worried about *my* job being dangerous?"

Two paws suddenly appeared on my bed. Mike obviously sensed the discord between Jay and me. "I'm trained to handle this sort of thing," I said.

"Which is what I've been trying to tell you about *my* job."

I stroked Mike's head, and she immediately went into her tail-wagging frenzy. I tried to reassure her I was okay. "I'll bet you're hungry," I said.

"I put down fresh food and water after I let her out. She ate a big breakfast and fed her litter."

"Thanks."

"You're welcome."

Our gazes met. We simply looked at each other. "I need to grab a shower," I said, wanting to feel the hot water on my aching body again. "It won't take me long to get ready." I brushed the covers aside and put my feet on the floor.

Jay covered my cast with the plastic bag once more. He slowly pulled me to my feet, and I suddenly found my body flush against his: chest to chest, thigh to thigh. I looked up. His face was only inches from mine. Again our gazes locked. I held my breath and waited.

"Katie?"

"Thank you for coming to the hospital and for staying with me, Jay," I said, trying to keep my voice steady and maybe a little impersonal because I felt too crummy to add to my already complicated life. "I owe you."

Something in his eyes changed. "No problem." Finally he stepped back.

Mona had the phone tucked between her jaw and shoulder, and was scribbling furiously on a sheet of paper when I walked through the door. To an innocent bystander it would appear she was hard at work, but I only had to see the Gucci catalog to know that she was placing an order. She looked up long enough to give a meaningful nod toward my office.

I almost dreaded what I might find. I walked inside and found Thad reclining on my sofa, reading my latest copy of *Psychology Today*.

chapter 10

·····················

As usual, Thad was immaculately dressed. He looked up, took me in from head to toe, and shook his head. "You don't look so good, Kate. Heard you broke your wrist," he added. "I hope that's not the hand you use for you-know-what." He gave me a hearty wink.

I put my pocketbook on my desk and leaned against it. "How was the fishing trip?"

He shuddered. "I'm still trying to get the smell of fish off my hands, but Thomas has decided not to sue Lucille for killing his hog. That is one mean woman. Could you imagine giving somebody like that the Rorschach test?"

"Thanks for taking my calls."

Thad tossed the magazine aside and stood. He pulled

a couple of slips of paper from the inside pocket of his jacket. "Nobody threatened to leap off a bridge or anything while you were unconscious, but this lady Alice Smithers—" He gave me a look. "Sounds like a candidate for shock therapy. Fortunately I was able to use my great skill and charm to calm her down. She was a different woman by the time we hung up."

"She's going through a difficult time," I said.

"Aren't they all?" He handed me the messages. "I've put in two calls to Harold Fry, but he hasn't called me back."

"I'm concerned about him," I said.

Thad shrugged. "He may be delusional at times, but he's not dangerous."

"You didn't have to drive all the way over to give these to me," I said, indicating the pink message slips. "You could have saved a lot of time by calling."

Thad straightened his tie. "I figured I'd better check on you and see how badly you were hurt," he said. "You look tired, Kate. You need a vacation, time to recuperate. And I know just the place."

"Yeah?"

"A friend of mine has an exclusive spa less than three hours from here. In-room body massages, facials and wraps, and a world-renowned chef. A weekend of pampering, and you'll be good as new. We could leave early this afternoon and drive back tomorrow night. That way I could beg off shooting skeet with Thomas."

"It sounds great, Thad," I said, "but I can't. My schedule is all screwed up after yesterday. And I'd really like to find Harold."

"The cops will call us when Harold decides to get naked in a parking lot someplace."

"I still can't go away with you, Thad," I said.

He shook his head sadly. "You used to be a lot of fun, Kate."

I waited until I'd heard him leave through the reception room door before I ventured out of my office. I found Mona wearing a neck brace. I just looked at her. "Okay, I give up. What's with the brace?"

"I have an appointment with that hot new chiropractor on the sixth floor. Dr. Dan Manning," she added. "The women refer to him as Dan the Man. I borrowed the brace from Mrs. Perez's son-in-law, who suffered whiplash in an automobile accident. It's my prop."

"Why do you need a prop?"

"There are women going to him who are perfectly healthy. The guy isn't an idiot. I'll have to convince him I'm really injured, you know?"

"What happens if he discovers there's nothing wrong with you?" I asked.

"I'll think of something. I always do." She looked at the clock on the wall. "Uh-oh, I don't want to be late for my appointment," she said, standing and grabbing her purse. "Don't worry about the phones; Nancy said she'll answer them."

"Um, Mona?"

She turned and glanced, questioning.

"Do you think I'm not as fun as I used to be?" I asked.

"You were more fun before you had your heart ripped apart." She hurried out.

Good old Mona. I could always count on her to make me feel better.

I returned Alice Smithers's call and agreed to see her at six p.m., which meant a long day. Then I noted that Cynthia Reed was due in an hour. When she arrived, she was holding a manila envelope. At least I saw nothing to indicate that she'd sneaked off to another plastic surgeon since her last visit. She noted my cast right away.

"I tripped and fell on my wrist," I said. "It's no big deal."

"Will you have a scar?" she asked. "I can give you the name of an excellent cosmetic surgeon."

"No scar," I assured her and motioned her to the sofa.

"I wrote the letter to my father like you suggested," she said once we were seated. "I told him how all those years of his watching everything my mom and I put in our mouths and making us weigh in every week made us feel bad about ourselves."

"Did it help?"

Her eyes filled with tears. "I cried a lot. I didn't realize how hurt I've been for so long."

"Do you feel like reading the letter to me?" I asked Cynthia.

She nodded and pulled a sheaf of pages from the envelope. I eyed the thick stack and wondered how many pages she had actually written.

"I wrote fourteen pages, front and back," she said, as though reading my mind. "I didn't want to leave out anything." She cleared her throat. " 'Dear Asshole,' " she began.

It took Cynthia the entire session to read her letter because she paused several times to cry. "I'm really proud of you for taking the time to write to your father," I said. "How do you feel?"

"I feel good about getting it off my chest, but I'm still angry at him. I want to tell him how I feel, because—" She paused in thought.

"Because you want him to apologize and validate your feelings," I said.

She nodded. "Right."

"What if he doesn't apologize?" I asked. "What if he pulls what you refer to as his pouting routine?" Cynthia looked uncertain. "I'm not saying you shouldn't confront him, but that is no guarantee that it will turn out the way you want."

I'd seen victims of all sorts of abuse confront those who'd hurt them. Although it worked well for the most part, I'd also watched abusers accuse their victims of lying or of making a big deal out of nothing. I'd watched them make excuses or blame others, and I'd watched them storm out of my office, outraged.

"What do you think I should do?" Cynthia asked.

"I think it's perfectly reasonable to confront somebody who has hurt you," I said, "and I hope you get what you feel you need. But you should be prepared. In the end it might come down to the fact that *you* have to love and accept yourself for who you are. It's your opinion that counts."

"I think I can do that," Cynthia said, "but I still want him to know that what he did was wrong. And the sooner the better," she added.

I reached for my appointment book.

Mona was back at her desk, wearing the brace, when I led Cynthia from my office. "What happened to your neck?" Cynthia said. "Were you and Dr. Kate in the same accident?"

"Not exactly," Mona said.

"I've scheduled Miss Reed to come in at three o'clock on Monday," I said, quickly changing the subject. "I want to make sure you haven't penciled anyone else in."

"Three o'clock is good," Mona said, entering it in the appointment book she kept. She jotted the time down on one of my cards and handed it to Cynthia.

I waited until Mona and I were alone before I asked about her appointment with Dan the Man.

163

"Oh, Kate," she whispered. "The guy is to die for. He has these chocolate eyes, and he smells sooo good. And guess what? I caught him looking at my legs twice."

"And he's single, huh?"

"Oh, yeah. That's the first thing I looked for. No wedding ring, no pictures of a wife and kids. Of course, he makes up for it. He has pictures of his golden Labrador retriever everywhere."

"What was his diagnosis with regard to your injury?"

"We just talked today. I'm scheduled to come in Monday for X-rays." She suddenly frowned. "I wish you could have seen all the sluts sitting in his waiting room, not a darn thing wrong with them. I can't wait till Monday. I'm going to buy a new outfit just for the occasion."

Mona had at least ten outfits for every occasion that existed, including Groundhog Day.

"So do you want to go to the mall tomorrow?" she asked.

I drove home at lunch to let Mike out, and found a petition on my door, signed by Bitsy Stout and about fifty others, no doubt members of her church. They were demanding that I remove the pornographic sculpture from my flower bed or face legal action. I decided I wasn't going to let it ruin my day, and I went inside, where Mike was doing what appeared to be a bumblebee mating dance at the back door. I quickly let her out.

I put the petition aside and checked on the puppies,

then called the vet's office and, because of a cancellation, was able to get an appointment for the following morning. I let Mike in and spent a few minutes of quality time with her before she climbed back into her box to nurse her babies.

Alice Smithers did not look well when she came in at the end of the day, although I saw one improvement. She wore different glasses, and they were actually flattering. As she stepped past me, I caught a whiff of tobacco, which surprised me because I had no idea she smoked.

"Something terrible has happened," she said once she was seated. "My roommate didn't pay me as promised."

"Oh no," I said.

Alice pressed her hands against her cheeks. "It gets worse. I called the restaurant where she said she worked. They've never heard of a Liz Jones."

"Oh no," I repeated.

"It gets even worse than that, if you can believe it," Alice said. "While I'm sitting on my sofa, trying to figure out what to do, Roy, the boyfriend, lets himself in the front door as though the place belongs to him. Liz obviously gave him the key to *my* condo!"

I could see that Alice was on the verge of losing it, and I didn't blame her. Just listening to her was like watching a bad soap opera. "What did you do?"

"Well, I freaked out. I demanded my key back, and I

told him to get out. And guess what he did? He laughed at me. He laughed and accused me of being a nutcase. Finally I told him I was calling the police, and he left."

"Did you get your key back?"

"Yes, thank God! He tossed it on the table before he walked out."

"You should probably consider having your locks changed, Alice."

"It's the original key," she said. "It wasn't a copy."

"Yes, but you don't know that a copy wasn't made."

"It's an old building with old locks. You can't just run up to Wal-Mart and get a copy made. I had to go to a hardware store. Liz and Roy don't strike me as people who'd go to that much trouble." She gave a sudden shiver. "Roy has probably been hanging out at my place while I've been at work. He probably doesn't even have a job."

"This really isn't my area of expertise, Alice," I said. "I don't know if you should be talking to the police or to a lawyer, but it sounds like you've got a couple of troublemakers on your hands."

"If Liz returns, she's going to find her clothes in a box outside the front door. Once Roy left, I went into Liz's room, *after* I used an ice pick to unlock the door, and you would not believe what I saw. The room was trashed. There were spills on the rug and cigarette butts everywhere! It smelled like a giant ashtray in there. And I specifically told her that she could not smoke inside because I have allergies."

"I thought I smelled smoke on you when you came through the door," I said. "It must've been from handling her things."

Alice nodded. "I didn't have time to grab a shower, because I was on my lunch hour and had to get back to the office."

"What are you going to do if she knocks on your door?" I asked.

Alice shrugged. "I'm not going to answer it, and if she doesn't go away, I'll call the police."

"How's your job search going?"

"I have an interview on Monday. I'm praying it goes well."

I sat there for a moment, taking it all in. Just hearing about Alice's life was exhausting. "How are you managing with all this stress, Alice?" I asked. "I know it has to be weighing heavily on you."

Her eyes filled with tears, and she pulled off her glasses. Again I was reminded what an attractive woman she really was. "I'm taking it one day at a time," she said. "I wish I hadn't bought my condo. I should have waited. I should have stayed in my little rental and saved more money. Now I'm financially strapped. I'm an accountant; I know better. That's what I get for acting on impulse."

She mopped her eyes. Her hands trembled, and she dropped her glasses. I reached for them and handed them to her. "I like your new glasses, by the way," I said.

She eyed them for a moment. "I'd forgotten I even

had them. I'm lucky if I can find my way home these days; that's how bad my memory is. I walk around feeling dazed at times. I glance up at the clock, and I'm shocked to discover what time it is. I'm just not *with it* right now, you know?"

"Stress does that." I waited until she seemed calmer. "Okay, listen," I said, falling back on my role as a therapist. "You've been dealing with a lot of stuff. Too much stuff," I added.

"Do you think I'm crazy?" she blurted.

Her question caught me off guard. "No, I don't think you're crazy. Why do you ask?"

"It's just the way Roy talked to me," she said. "Like I was some insane person or something," she added. "He made fun of me."

"How do you expect him to act? He was trying to mooch off you, and you confronted him. That's what happens when you confront people who are trying to use or abuse you. They sometimes get nasty. But what is your alternative?"

"Being a doormat," she said.

"I'm really proud of you for standing up for yourself, Alice," I told her, "but you need to ward off this sort of thing in the future by being more cautious and assertive where people are concerned. You have to put firm boundaries in place or people will continue to take advantage of you. We can work on that."

Alice shifted uncomfortably on the sofa. "Dr. Holly—" She paused. "I mean, Kate. I can't really afford therapy."

More tears, a quick laugh. "I probably need a ton of it, but I just don't have the money right now."

I sat there quietly. This is where I often get myself into trouble. I see a person in pain, and the thought of paying my electric bill flies right out the door. "I've been known to take some cases pro bono, Alice."

"Oh, I could never do that."

"You could pay me later. Or you could make small payments when you are able. It doesn't matter. What matters is getting you healthy." I had real reasons for wanting Alice to keep coming to me. That she had admitted to being a doormat, that she had such low self-esteem and hadn't the first clue about setting boundaries, smacked of childhood abuse. It would not be easy getting her to open up: children of abuse learned at a very young age to keep secrets.

"I'll think about it," Alice said.

chapter 11

....

A block from my house, I saw my mother and aunt turning in to my driveway. I parked beside them a moment later and found them pulling boxes from the back of their monster truck.

"We have dishes and cookware and everything else you could possibly need for your kitchen!" my mother said, excitement and pride lighting her face. It faded quickly, and her eyes widened. "What happened to your wrist?"

"I fell and fractured it," I said with a shrug. "I'm fine."

"Did you have to go to the emergency room?"

"Only briefly," I said, knowing my mother would freak if I told her I'd actually undergone surgery without calling her. "It's a minor injury."

"I hope you weren't drinking when you fell," she said. "You know what a problem we had with Uncle Bump. You can't be too careful, since you probably inherited his genes."

I looked at Aunt Trixie, who shook her head in sympathy for me. "I'm trying really hard to stay on the straight and narrow these days, Mom." I started to take the box from her, but she shooed me away.

"You shouldn't be lifting things with a broken wrist. Just unlock the door and let us inside."

I stabbed my key in my lock and pushed the door open. Mike rushed out happily to greet me. I heard a scream and turned, just as my mother let go of the box. It hit the ground with a thud—but fortunately I didn't hear anything shatter.

"Whose dog is that?" my mother cried as she climbed inside the truck and slammed the door.

"She's mine, and she's harmless," I said.

"Don't you know I was almost mauled to death by a dog?" She held her thumb and forefinger an inch apart. "I came *this close* to dying."

"You didn't almost die," Aunt Trixie said. "I was there, remember? Stop acting like a nincompoop and get out of the truck."

I leaned forward and picked up Mike. "Look, Mom," I said. "She's very friendly. And she has puppies. You should see them; they're adorable."

"Could you make me a cup of coffee?" Aunt Trixie asked. "Well, never mind—you do have a broken wrist.

I'll put on a pot. I need a good caffeine kick after hanging out at an estate sale this afternoon. Let your mother sit out in the truck if she likes."

It was unlike Aunt Trixie to get annoyed, but she could get as irritated with my mother as the next person could, especially if she was tired.

"We're going inside for coffee, Mom," I said. "Feel free to join us, okay?"

The coffee was already poured by the time my mother came into the house. "Where is that hound of Satan?"

"She's in the laundry room eating her young," I said. "Would you like a cup of coffee?"

"I suppose," she said grudgingly.

The telephone rang. I picked it up. There was no answer, only breathing. I hung up.

"Who was that?" my mother asked.

I checked the caller ID and was not surprised to find that the number was unavailable. "My neighbor has been on my case about the sculpture," I said. I handed my mother the petition. "You've heard me mention Bitsy Stout?"

"The religious zealot from across the street?" Aunt Trixie asked.

"That's the one. She and, it seems, other church members find it offensive."

My mother read the petition. "She's full of hot air. Take a look, Trixie." She handed it to my aunt.

"Maybe you should just ignore her," Aunt Trixie said once she finished looking it over.

I had no intention of telling either of them exactly what I'd been through over the statue.

The phone rang again. I didn't bother to pick it up.

Jay's voice came on my answering machine. "Hi, Katie," he said in his toe-curling voice. "Just checking to see if you're okay and if you need me to spend the night again," he said. "I can make you forget your pain. I can wear those boxer shorts you bought me with the big red lips. You know how you love those boxers. Give me a call."

My mother's mouth formed an O of surprise. "Jay spent the night here?"

"It's not what you think."

"You should return his call," my mother said before I could explain. "I think he'd take you back if you asked nicely."

I smiled grimly, determined not to let her get me riled. "You think?"

Mike suddenly reappeared and sniffed my mother's ankles. She jumped and almost spilled her coffee. "We should be going, Trixie," she said.

"Not till I see the puppies," my aunt told her as she hurried into the laundry room. Mike followed her, tail wagging.

My mother gave a grunt. "You bought that dog so I would stay away, didn't you? Admit it."

"That's the most ridiculous thing I've ever heard, Mom. Nobody in their right mind would shell out good money for a mutt with wiry hair."

I waited until I heard the Junk Sisters pull away in their big truck before I returned Jay's call. He picked up on the second ring. "My mom and my aunt loved the message you left," I said.

He chuckled. "I like playing to an audience. How are you? I tried to call you at the office earlier in the day, but you were with a patient."

"It was a madhouse. No pun intended," I added.

"Have you eaten yet?"

"I just finished, as a matter of fact," I lied, knowing I didn't need to see him. "Listen, I really appreciate your babysitting last night, but I'm fine now."

"Was that a brush-off?" he asked.

"I have a lot of stuff to do," I said, "and I'm really tired. And one of my patients is missing, and I need to try to find him."

Silence at first. "Tell you what, Katie," Jay said after a moment. "How about I back off? That way I don't have to beat my head against a brick wall trying to figure out what you want or don't want from me."

We hung up. I stood there for a moment, trying to swallow the mammoth-sized lump in my throat. I checked the puppies and put a clean towel in the box. They were cute little buggers. I picked up the runt and studied him. It bothered me that he didn't seem to be gaining weight like the others, and he wasn't as active.

I put him down and picked up one of the larger pups and held him to my ear, listening to the grunting sound he made and shivering when he took my earlobe in his mouth, obviously mistaking it for his mother's nipple. Sometimes little things like that can make a world of difference when you're hurting inside.

After a few moments I returned the squirming puppy to his siblings, and he scrambled between their furry, warm bodies. I gave Mike fresh food and water and handed her a dog biscuit, which she gobbled.

I popped a frozen chicken pot pie in the microwave, and went upstairs to change into baggy jeans. Back in the kitchen, I ate my pot pie and dubiously regarded the boxes of dishes and cookware. I remembered the promise I had made to myself to start eating healthful food.

I finished my dinner and checked the time. Saturday night, eight p.m. What did an almost-divorced woman do on a Saturday night? How many times had I asked myself that question? I had dreaded the weekends with all my heart when I first left Jay. Weekends with Jay had been spectacular, filled with yummy sex, bubble baths, steamy showers, breakfast in bed, and more yummy sex.

I could feel a pity party coming on, and that annoyed the hell out of me, since I had officially given them up after the night Mona and I had spent drinking too much wine beside her pool. I'd ended up with the mother of all hangovers and a resolve to stop whining and start living again.

The psychologist in me stepped forward. Okay, so I had experienced a huge emotional slip, brought on by the night I'd spent in Jay's bed and the night he'd spent in mine taking care of me. Why did love have to hurt so much? Even worse was knowing that I had the power to stop that hurt.

I could call Jay and he would be here in twenty minutes, and in a matter of hours I'd be moving out of Mad Ethel, with her plumbing problems and ugly kitchen.

And I'd be right back where I started. Back to worrying 24-7 about Jay, back to questioning his every move, watching him close down on me, and feeling the relationship slip away.

Either way, it hurt.

I sat at the table, drumming my fingers. If I had a patient in such a predicament, I would tell her to get involved in something that would make her feel better. Start a project, maybe.

My eyes automatically went to the kitchen walls and their outdated wallpaper. Anybody would be depressed living in a house with such an ugly kitchen. After all, the kitchen was the heart of the home. I tried to imagine coming home at the end of the day to an attractive kitchen, and I got a good feeling just thinking about it.

I tried to think of all I knew about removing wallpaper, and came up with zero. Fortunately the large home improvement store not far from me not only of-

fered classes but their employees were also fairly helpful. How hard could it be?

I walked into the laundry room and announced to
Mike my decision to redo the kitchen. She stood in her
box and wagged her tail with great enthusiasm. By the
time I climbed into my car a few minutes later, I was
convinced I was on the right track.

Inside the store, I quickly grabbed a shopping cart
and searched the aisles for the wallpaper section. Although Mona claimed hardware and home improvement
stores were a great place to meet men, I figured most
men *worth* dating would be *on* a date, seeing as how it
was Saturday night. Which didn't say much for me as a
woman, since I was there; plus, I couldn't imagine Mona
being in a hardware store to begin with.

A high school kid who could have passed for Richie
Cunningham of *Happy Days* was restocking shelves in
the paint and wallpaper department.

"I want to strip wallpaper from my kitchen wall," I
announced.

He nodded. "Have you ever done it before?"

"Nope."

"Uh-oh."

"I don't expect it to be fun," I said.

"What kind of paper is it?"

"It's an old house. No telling how long the paper has
been up."

"Is it vinyl?"

"No."

"Uh-oh."

"Look, I know I can do it. I just need instructions."

"You'll need a scoring tool," he said. He led me to a shelf and picked up something that resembled a door-knob with notched teeth on the underside. He explained how it worked to perforate the paper. Then he reached for a plastic container of wallpaper gel. "You use a paintbrush or roller to apply this gel to the paper, and you let it sit for maybe half an hour before you start scraping. You may have to repeat the steps several times. After that, you'll want to sand over the whole thing."

"That doesn't sound so bad," I said.

He shrugged. "I suppose there are worse things."

I put the items in my cart and pushed it toward the wallpaper samples. There were dozens of patterns from which to choose, and I got excited just thinking about my new kitchen. "I'll come back in a few days and se-lect the paper," I said.

"Have you ever put up wallpaper?"

"No."

"Uh-oh."

I was on my third pot of coffee—if I took it slow, I could manage it with my wrist in a cast—and the morn-ing sun was peeking through the curtains by the time I'd reached the bare walls in my kitchen. I had worked through the night. My hair was sticky with the wallpaper-removal gel, and I had several thin strips of paper plastered to my cast, my arms, and my bare legs.

I heard the click of Mike's toenails as she entered the room and looked about. She had come in several times during the night to watch. Since I'd already been up, I had checked on the runt and made sure he nursed every couple of hours.

"What do you think?" I asked Mike. "A little more sanding here and there, and I'll be finished."

Her tail did a little wag before she made her way to the back door. I let her out. While I waited, I slumped in a chair at the kitchen table, crossed my arms, and put my head down. I was bone tired. Stripping wallpaper, especially with only one hand, is no picnic. I had no idea why I'd chosen to work all night. Probably because the job had sucked so bad that I figured if I stopped, I'd never get back to it. Or maybe I was so desperate to start feeling better about my life that I was just clinging to anything that might bring a ray of hope my way.

You used to be a lot of fun, Kate.

I closed my eyes. I knew Thad was right. Despite my shaky formative years, I'd managed to emerge optimistic and eager about my future. I'd derived great pleasure from helping people.

In my brief marriage, I'd joined other firefighters' wives in various fund-raising schemes, and I attended every social function, be it a bridal or baby shower, a barbecue, or the annual Christmas party. Jay's friends, and their wives and kids, had become like family. Several of the wives had continued to call after Jay and I split. We could have remained friends, but I sadly let them go. I didn't want to be reminded of all I'd lost.

Maybe I *wasn't* a barrel of laughs at the moment, but the deep-down sense of optimism remained. I would get through this.

When I opened my eyes, the kitchen was bathed in light, and my back and shoulders were stiff and sore. I blinked several times as I stretched and tried to work out the kinks. I looked at the clock. It was after eight. Eight! Holy crap, I was supposed to have Mike and her pups at the vet's office at eight thirty. Where the heck was Mike?

I jumped up, raced to the back door, and threw it open. Mike was lying spread-eagled in a patch of sun. She opened her eyes and wagged her tail, but didn't make a move to get up.

"What are you doing?" I demanded. "We're supposed to be at the vet's office in fifteen minutes! How come you didn't wake me? How come you're out here sunbathing when you have a boxful of puppies to take care of? Why am I even talking to you?"

In response, Mike rolled over, got to her feet, and gave a good shake before heading inside. I grabbed the phone book and searched frantically for Midtown Veterinary Clinic.

I dialed the number quickly. My fingernails were stuffed with wallpaper gunk. A woman answered, and I wasted no time.

"This is Kate Holly, and I have an appointment to see

Dr. Henry at eight thirty, and I just woke up. Could I reschedule for later in the day?"

"We're only here until noon, Ms. Holly," the woman said, "and there isn't another time available. Would you like something for next week?"

"I can't wait that long."

"What would you like to do, Ms. Holly?" the voice asked.

I knew I looked like a nightmare, but I couldn't risk missing the appointment. I needed to have the vet examine the little runt. "Okay," I said quickly, talking more to myself than her. "I may be five or ten minutes late, but I'll be there."

I hung up and hurried to the bathroom. I tried not to shriek at my own reflection. There was no time for a shower. I washed my face and hands, and tried to comb some of the gel from my hair. I raced up the stairs, changed into jeans, and pulled on my sneakers.

Downstairs, I tucked my purse beneath my arm and ran into the laundry room, where I shooed Mike from the box. "You should have thought about feeding your children while you were out sunbathing," I said crossly. "Now you've made us late."

It seemed to take forever to get us all in the car, which gave me a new respect for parents who are able to get their children fed, dressed, and at school before lunchtime each day.

We were fifteen minutes late for our appointment, but the young receptionist was nice about it. I don't know whether it was due to the desperation on my face or whether she felt embarrassed for any woman who would go out in public looking like I did.

She grabbed a clipboard and led me to one of the examination rooms. Mike followed.

"I just need to ask a couple of questions before Dr. Henry comes in," she said. "You can put the box on the exam table."

Mike nudged me several times as I rattled off my name, address, and phone number; I suddenly realized she must be anxious over her puppies. I picked her up and put her in the box with them.

"What is your dog's name and age?" the girl asked.

"Her name is Mike. She's a stray, so I have no idea how old she is. Correction—she *was* a stray before I let her in and she had puppies in my laundry room."

"Sounds like we have a Good Samaritan on our hands," a man said from the doorway.

I glanced over my shoulder and saw a hunk in a white lab coat. He smiled and took the clipboard from the receptionist.

"I'm Dr. Jeff Henry." He offered his hand.

I laughed self-consciously. "You don't want to shake hands with me. I've been stripping wallpaper all night."

He chuckled. "Afraid I'll stick to you?"

I smiled, but the thought of him sticking to me made my stomach quiver. "This is Mike," I said, "and these are her offspring. They were born in the wee morning hours last Tuesday."

Dr. Henry patted Mike on the head. "I take it this was an unplanned pregnancy?"

I shrugged. "I don't know the details, but I'm pretty sure it was the result of a one-night stand."

He looked at Mike and grinned. "And you look like such a nice, respectable girl." He stroked Mike with one hand and gently lifted each puppy. He examined them quickly, took their temperatures, clipped their dew claws, and weighed them. "Are they staying nice and warm?" he asked.

"Yes, there's a heating pad in the box."

He nodded, then frowned once he weighed the runt. "This little fellow might not make it."

I heard myself gasp. "Oh no!"

Dr. Henry looked at me, and his expression became gentle. His eyes were liquid brown. "I'm sorry. Not all puppies survive, even under the best conditions. Since this mother was probably a stray like you say, there's no way to know if she was eating regularly, although she doesn't look malnourished." He placed the puppy in the palm of his hand and pulled the skin away from the back of his neck and watched it. "Is he nursing as often as the others, do you know?"

"A friend has been helping me see that he nurses as much as possible."

"He should be placed on a teat before the others, but as long as he is interested in nursing, let's not make any changes. If he doesn't gain over the next couple of days, or if he loses interest and becomes lethargic, I can show you how to tube-feed him. That's really about all you can do, to be perfectly honest."

He put the runt down and checked Mike's eyes and teeth before running his hands through her fur and finally looking at her nails. "She hasn't had a lot of attention, and she definitely needs to be on vitamins." He thumped her stomach lightly and listened with his stethoscope, then took her temperature. Mike sat through it quietly. "What do you plan to do with them?"

"I don't know. I don't want to take them to the shelter."

He nodded. "It's a hard decision," he said. "Mike will need to be tested for parasites and go on heartworm medication. She'll need the usual bout of shots. You'll want to have her spayed." He looked at me. "It can get expensive, and that doesn't include worming and vaccinating the puppies."

"Good thing I'm filthy rich, huh?" I said dully.

He smiled. "I have a feeling that if you were filthy rich, you would have let someone else spend the night stripping off your wallpaper."

"I'm sort of taking it one day at a time," I said after a moment, "although I think I've found a home for one of them once they're weaned."

"You can take a picture of them in a couple of weeks and put it on the bulletin board in the waiting room," he suggested. "Since you're not a breeder, I'll give them their worm medicine and shots at cost when it's time, and I won't charge you for their exams."

His gaze was warm and compassionate, and I could tell he liked his job and took it seriously. "Thank you, Dr. Henry."

"Jeff."

My gaze automatically went to his ring finger. I wanted to be able to give Mona the goods on the man. There was no wedding band.

He finished up. "Why don't you touch base with me in a couple of days, let me know how the runt is doing. Or you can wrap him in a towel and bring him by, and I'll weigh him."

I felt eager about coming back, and wondered whether my broken heart was beginning to heal or whether I was just hopeful, desperate, or downright pathetic. Jeff carried the box to my car while I paid the bill. I asked myself whether he was just a supergreat vet or whether he was mildly interested in me. One look in the rearview mirror at my gunk-filled hair and unmade-up face convinced me he had acted out of pure sympathy.

chapter 12

....

I'd showered and taken a two-hour nap when the phone rang. Mona was ready to hit the mall. My job was to help her carry the shopping bags. I was willing to do this from time to time because she worked for me for free.

"I'll go, but only if Mrs. Perez can check on the puppies every couple of hours until we get back. Somebody has to make sure Runt nurses."

"Runt? You actually named him Runt? Won't that give him a complex?"

"His ears aren't open yet," I told her. "Maybe I'll come up with something new before he's able to hear."

"Mrs. Perez has already agreed to babysit," Mona assured me. "I can tell she's really attached to Mike and the puppies. She might be able to help you find homes for them."

"That's great," I said, knowing Mrs. Perez would be very selective.

"So how soon can you be ready?"

I arrived at Mona's an hour later, wearing one of my nicest outfits and comfortable shoes. Mona's choice of malls was Phipps Plaza. Not only is it in ritzy Buckhead, but it is considered the premier place to shop and has all of Mona's favorite stores under one roof: Nordstrom, Saks Fifth Avenue, Gucci, Giorgio, and other such exclusive shops. There is an unspoken dress code at Phipps Plaza: you do not want to arrive in cutoff jeans and flip-flops.

That's why I'm partial to Wal-Mart. At Wal-Mart nobody cares if some guy leaning over to study hammers is showing three inches of butt crack. All shoppers are created equal at Wal-Mart, as long as their credit cards are good.

Phipps Plaza offers a Cadillac valet service at the main entrance. For a nominal fee they'll park your car and retrieve it. If you're driving a Cadillac, the service is free. Mona insists on using the limo because it is, after all, head and shoulders above a Cadillac.

Over lunch, I told Mona how I'd spent my evening and about meeting Dr. Jeff Henry.

A look of disbelief crossed her face. "You actually went to his office covered in wallpaper goop? Why didn't you reschedule?"

"I was worried about Runt, and I'd missed the first appointment when I had to go to the ER. Besides, I didn't know the man was going to be gorgeous," I added.

"Wedding band?"

"No."

"Are you interested?"

"No. That's why I'm giving *you* the goods on him. I just like looking at the man, you know?"

Mona seemed to ponder it. "I think I'll stick with the chiropractor for now. I don't want to have to go out and buy a dog in case you discover you like this guy after all. Although—" She paused. "I suppose I could borrow my neighbor's Lhasa apso and check him out. I need a really sexy breed to take in, you know? The breed of dog says a lot about the owner."

"Then I'm screwed," I said, thinking of Mike and her unattractive coat. At the same time, I couldn't believe the conversation we were having. Dr. Jeff Henry probably already had a girlfriend.

Five hours and an armload of shopping bags later, I managed to point to my wristwatch. "I need to head back," I said. My lack of sleep the night before was starting to catch up with me.

Mona still had the glazed look in her eyes that told me she had not yet satisfied her need to touch raw silk and high-quality linen. She gave a heartfelt sigh but whipped out her cell phone to notify her chauffeur she was ready for him to pick us up.

We arrived back at Mona's. As I was climbing from

the limo, she reached inside one of her shopping bags and pulled out a smaller one. "This is for you."

"You didn't have to do this," I said, touched that Mona had gotten me the entire gift set of my favorite Donna Karan perfume. She had introduced me to it the previous Christmas.

"You earned it," Mona said.

I returned to the hardware store and found the red-haired kid sweeping. He recognized me right away.

"How did it go?" he asked. "Were you able to get the wallpaper off?"

"Yes, but I will never put myself through that again. I was hoping you could give me the name of someone who could put the new paper up for me. Preferably somebody affordable," I added.

"Uh-oh." The kid had a limited vocabulary.

"Is it really expensive?"

"It's not cheap. Plus, the good installers usually have more work than they can keep up with. You might have to go on a waiting list."

I wondered how long I could live with bare walls. "Okay. I'll leave my phone number with you. I should probably pick out my paper now."

He stepped closer. "I'm not supposed to tell you this, but we're having a sale next week on our stock merchandise. Thirty percent off," he added. "Trust me, you have plenty of time."

"It sounds like I could get a doctor's appointment quicker," I mumbled.

"Yeah, but I'll bet your doctor doesn't know how to put up wallpaper."

chapter 13

·····································

I arrived at my office the next morning to find Mona dressed to the nines and wearing her neck brace. "I have to see my chiropractor this morning for X-rays," she said. "I was up half the night with a backache. I think it's from my neck injury."

"But you don't really have a neck injury, Mona," I reminded her.

"It's this brace. I think it did something to my alignment. Nancy is going to grab the phone while I'm out."

I went inside my office and called Thad. "I still haven't heard from Harold Fry," I said. "I've called his place, and I stopped by the McDonald's where he always eats breakfast. He wasn't there."

"Tell me you're wearing a thong today," Thad said, his voice almost pleading.

"Did you hear what I just said? Harold Fry is still MIA!"

"I don't care about Harold right now, okay? Could we talk about *me* for once?"

I rolled my eyes. "For once?" I repeated.

"I went to all-night bowling with Thomas on Saturday. We drank warm beer and sat next to women who don't shave their armpits. I'm pretty sure that's where Thomas met Lucille."

Thad sounded depressed. "Maybe you're overdoing it," I suggested. "All I said was that you should spend some time with him. You don't have to move in together." Okay, so maybe I'd said a little more than that, I thought. But I'd been annoyed with Thad at the time for getting me involved in a family dispute. I had enough of that going on in my own family.

"We're supposed to see *Spider-Man 3* tonight. I need your help, Kate."

"I'm not going to volunteer to go see *Spider-Man 3* in your place," I said. "I haven't seen one and two yet."

"I want you to convince Thomas to go back to Lucille."

"What! You can't mean that. The woman is a sociopath."

"She was just angry. I've had women threaten to do worse than that to me, trust me."

"Threatening to do something and actually doing it are two different things, Thad."

"A woman once threatened to cut off my you-know-what and stuff it down my throat," Thad said.

"That was me," I told him. "I said that when I caught you and your receptionist in your hot tub, naked."

"That was *you*! Wow, how did that slip my memory?"

Obviously Thad had been threatened for cheating by more than one woman. "Remember? I changed my mind because I couldn't find a dull knife."

Thad gave a heavy sigh. "I know I'm being driven by guilt to be with Thomas. I should have been a better brother to him."

"Try not to get so down on yourself," I said, having trouble believing I was saying those words to Thad Glazer. "At least this proves you have a conscience. Besides, your brother is a big boy, and he has a business to run. He'll understand if you're busy."

"I could tell Thomas you and I had dinner plans, and I forgot. That way I wouldn't have to hurt his feelings, and you and I could—"

"Sorry, but I can't have dinner with you." I saw movement in the doorway and was stunned to find Thomas, the subject of our conversation, standing there.

"I know all your favorite restaurants," Thad reminded me from the other end of the line.

"Um, someone just walked in my office. I have to go. In the meantime, you might try to figure out where Harold Fry is." I hung up the phone. "Thomas, what a surprise!" I said.

"I just need a minute of your time."

"Come in."

He stepped inside. "It's about Thad. I know he's concerned about me after I split up with Lucille, but he's driving me crazy. He thinks he has to spend every minute with me. I need some time to myself, you know. I'm sort of trying to pursue a new relationship."

As I listened, I realized that human beings were incapable of living simple, uncomplicated lives and relationships were rife with misunderstandings. It was so much easier hanging out with a wiry-haired dog whose only hang-up was that she sometimes licked her butt. I suddenly understood why Thomas's best friend had been a hog.

"Oops, I forgot to tell you. Alice Smithers called earlier," Mona said shortly after she returned from the chiropractor. I lay on my sofa with my eyes closed. "She wanted to see if you could work her in. You had a cancellation at two o'clock, so I put her down. Why are you lying down? Are you not feeling well? I knew you should have taken more time to heal before returning to work."

"I'm meditating," I said.

"Then it won't bother you if I sit in here and talk, right?" She took the chair beside the sofa.

"The object of meditation is to be silent," I told her.

"Oh, okay."

I took a deep calming breath.

"For how long?" Mona asked after a few minutes.

"However long it takes."

"Oh, okay."

A minute passed. Mona sighed.

"Is there something you wanted to discuss with me?" I asked.

"I wasn't going to tell you, but I'm afraid *not* to tell you. If I tell you, it's just going to stress you out, and probably nothing will come of it—"

I opened my eyes. "Mona?"

"But then if something bad happened, I would never forgive myself."

"Would you just *tell* me, for Pete's sake!"

"That guy called," she said. "The weird one," she added.

I just looked at her. "I know this sounds sad, but you're going to have to be more specific."

"The guy that accused you of being a troublemaker," she said.

"Just what I need."

"He got mad at me because I wouldn't pass him through to you. I told him you were in a session."

"What did he want?"

"He said he was giving you one more chance, but if you didn't stop making trouble, you were going to pay."

I felt the back of my neck prickle. "Did he have a speech impediment? A lisp?"

"Yes. I told him I was going to have his call traced and report him to the police, but he laughed at me and hung up. He was probably calling from a pay phone." She paused. "Do you think we should contact the police?"

"And tell them what?" I asked. "We don't know who the caller is."

"Of course we do. It's some nut from Bitsy's church," she said. "Maybe if the police went over and questioned people, it would scare him and he'd stop."

"I'll call Bitsy later and threaten to file a police report if she doesn't stop harassing me," I said. "For what it's worth," I added. I had a feeling I wasn't going to get any peace until the statue was gone.

I was surprised and delighted to find Alice Smithers wearing a fashionable outfit when she arrived. She'd even used blush. I could tell Mona was impressed. Unfortunately Alice didn't look happy. In fact, she looked mad as hell.

"Look at this!" she said, yanking a slip of paper from her purse. "It's my Visa bill."

I saw several charges for gasoline, one for books from a Barnes & Noble, and another for shoes. "Four hundred and fifty dollars for a pair of Prada high heels? Wow!" I said.

"Wow is right!" Alice said. "Liz stole my credit card. Are you believing that?"

"Actually, I'm stunned. Where on earth can you buy Prada heels for four hundred and fifty dollars?" I made a note of the store.

"Naturally, my card is still missing," Alice said.

"Did you report it?"

"Right away," she said. "I reported it to the police as well. And guess what else? Liz hasn't returned for her things. They were still sitting outside my door when I left for work this morning."

I was as surprised by Alice's anger as I was by her attire. "Good for you," I said, "for taking immediate action."

"I'm tired of people walking all over me, Kate. I can't believe I allowed my boss and his wife to treat me like they did. I told them I was going to an attorney."

"Really? What did they say?"

"They said I was making a serious mistake. They gave me this crap about how they have tried to be fair with me *under the circumstances*, whatever *that* means, but I didn't fall for one word of it. They're vultures, just like Liz and Roy." She leaned closer. "Of course, I can't really afford a lawyer, but they don't know that. I figured it would keep them off my butt until I find the job I deserve."

I felt like applauding the change in Alice's attitude. Gone was the doormat of a woman who had come to me previously. Even her posture had changed: shoulders thrown back, chin hitched high. "I'm so proud of you, Alice," I said, and meant it. "I know anger feels uncomfortable, but sometimes you have to allow yourself to experience it."

"I've been angry for a very long time," she said.

"Maybe all my life. I feel like it has been sitting just under the surface waiting to come out. Like a ticking time bomb," she added. "Oh, boy, I have to go," she said, checking her wristwatch.

"But you just got here."

"Yes, but I've been dealing with the police, and I need to get back to the office," she said. "Besides, I'm done."

"I don't think you are."

"What makes you say that?"

"There's a reason you've had problems standing up for yourself most of your life, Alice. A reason you haven't been able to set boundaries with people. It didn't happen overnight."

"I don't know why people like you try to make your patients feel bad about themselves," she blurted.

I was surprised by her words and tone. "That's not what I'm trying to do."

"You want to know why I have so many problems with relationships, and you're determined to dig and dig, and you don't care how much it hurts. Well, let me give you the short version. My mother is a big fat drunk who was never there for me. Is that what you want to hear, Kate?"

"I just want to help," I said, realizing I had just pushed past Alice's No Trespassing sign.

"She's in her late sixties now, and can't understand why I don't visit. If you want to find out what makes people do the things they do, call *her*."

I followed Alice into the reception area. She dropped a wad of cash onto Mona's desk and left without a word. "Looks like you botched that one," Mona said under her breath.

I ignored her and turned to where Arnie Decker, the ex-Marine, was waiting. He wore sandals, and his toenails were painted.

"I didn't realize we had an appointment today, Mr. Decker," I said.

"Oh, I'm not here for therapy," he said. "Nancy is giving me a manicure today."

I had just finished up with a patient and was going through my appointment book when Mona tapped on the door, stepped inside, and closed it behind her. She'd worn the neck brace all day and it was getting on my nerves, but, then, I was just having a bad day.

"Your aunt Lou is here to see you," she said. "And she's wearing one hundred percent polyester."

"Did she say what she wanted?" I asked.

"Nope."

I gave a monumental sigh and followed Mona into the reception room with a large fake smile plastered to my face. "Aunt Lou, what a surprise," I said.

"I need to talk to you, Kate," she said. Her smoker's voice made her sound as though her larynx had been raked over gravel. "It's personal." She looked at Mona. "No offense."

Mona smiled. "No problem."

"Sure, Aunt Lou." I motioned her inside my office and closed the door. I wondered whether Lucien had done something. He was always getting into some kind of trouble. Uncle Bump had called me for advice on more than one occasion. "Have a seat," I said.

She sat on my sofa. "This is very embarrassing. I hate going to doctors. I can't remember the last time I did."

She wore no makeup and her face was leathery, but Aunt Lou did not strike me as a woman who would care about face moisturizer. "What is it?" I asked.

"I'm miserable. I've got this damn itch inside my vagina."

"I'm sorry to hear that." Mostly I was sorry that I was forced to think about Aunt Lou's vagina.

"I'm sure it's a blasted yeast infection, but I've tried everything and I can't get rid of it. I've even tried yogurt."

"Did you say yogurt?"

"It's an old home remedy. Have you ever tried to scoop a whole container of yogurt into your vagina?"

"No, Aunt Lou, I haven't."

"Well, it's a bitch keeping the stuff in, let me tell you."

It was not an image I wanted to wrap my mind around. "So, how can I help you? I mean, I'm more than happy to listen, but—"

"I'd like for you to write me a prescription for something to stop this damn infernal itching."

"I can't write prescriptions."

"You're a *doctor*, for God's sake. People call you Dr. Holly. I've heard them."

"We've had this talk before, Aunt Lou," I said calmly, "when you had hemorrhoids."

"Yes, but that was before you got this fancy office and started seeing patients."

"You need an MD to prescribe medication."

"What the hell are you?"

"I'm a Ph.D. I have a doctorate in clinical psychology. I'm not licensed to practice medicine or write prescriptions."

"I know what this is about. You're thinking I don't plan to pay you. You think I'm looking for a handout."

"That thought never crossed my mind, Aunt Lou, but it doesn't change anything. You need a medical doctor. I'll be glad to give you the name of mine, but that's the best I do."

She didn't look happy. "I'm the one who talked Lucien into giving your mother a discount on her big party," she said, "and this is the thanks I get?"

She fumbled with the latch on her purse, and I feared she was reaching for her ice pick. Instead she pulled out her car keys. "I could maybe get you a free manicure while you're here," I said.

She stood. "I don't *need* a manicure. Sorry I *bothered* you," she said with a huff.

I walked her out. "How's Uncle Bump?"

She gave a grunt. "Don't get me started. You're lucky Jay left you when he did, because the older men get, the

201

needier they get. Remember that the next time you start feeling sorry for yourself."

"I will."

She looked at Mona. "I hope your neck gets better, young lady. Don't forget what I told you about using kerosene."

Mona smiled and tapped the side of her head. "I've got it stored right up here."

Aunt Lou gave me a hard look. "Just so you know, I'm going to try not to hold this against you, but I'm not making any promises." She opened the door and walked out.

"Uh-oh," Mona said. "What's with her?"

"You don't want to know." I started for my office and turned. "What's with the kerosene?"

"You don't want to know."

I figured we were both right.

chapter 14

·····························

Cynthia Reed and her father arrived at four thirty, wearing tense looks. As I greeted them, Mona handed me several phone messages.

"Harold Fry called?" I asked before joining Cynthia and her father inside my office. "What did he say? Did he tell you where he was? Did he leave a number?"

"No, but he promised to call back."

"If he does, put him through to me, even if I'm in a session."

Cynthia and her father took seats at opposite ends of the sofa. Mr. Reed was immaculately dressed in a form-fitting suit, a white dress shirt, and a gray tie. "Thank you for joining us today, Mr. Reed," I said, sitting in my usual chair. "Did Cynthia mention why she wanted you to be here?"

He looked at his daughter. "Only that she needed to talk to me with her therapist present. I didn't know she was seeing a therapist. Just plastic surgeons," he added with a sigh.

"Dad, don't start giving me a hard time, okay? It's my money." She crossed her arms. "That's not why I asked you to come."

"I'm concerned that you're getting obsessed, Doodlebug."

Cynthia threw up her arms in disgust and looked at me. "Did you hear what he just called me?"

Mr. Reed smacked his forehead. "I'm sorry, Cynthia." He looked at me. "I've been calling her that since, well, since she was an infant."

"Why did you choose that particular nickname for your daughter?" I asked.

He paused in thought. "Let me think." He suddenly smiled. "Now I remember. When Cynthia was a newborn, she used to draw her legs to her chest and curl into a tight ball." He chuckled. "We later learned it was gas, but she reminded me of a little doodlebug."

I saw that he had Cindy's undivided attention.

"Why did you wait until *now* to tell me that?" she demanded.

He looked confused. "You never asked."

"Dammit, Dad!" she said.

"What? It was a silly nickname. It made you giggle when you were a little girl. Then you turned twelve years old and hated it."

"When I was twelve, I was fat and wearing braces!" she said, picking up a throw pillow and hitting him with it.

Startled, he jumped. "You weren't fat! What has gotten into you?"

"I think we need to call a time-out," I said.

"Doodlebugs are fat," Cynthia said. "You made me feel fat. Why else would you have put everybody on a strict diet and exercise regimen if you didn't think I was fat?" She hit him with the pillow again. "You became a fanatic, insisting we watch everything we put in our mouths. Then every Monday we had to weigh in so you could record it."

"Cynthia, please don't hit your father with the pillow. Otherwise we're going to have to stop the session."

She ignored me and hit him again. "You were like a drill instructor!" she said. "I became so self-conscious, I started skipping lunch at school. I was starving myself! Starving!" she shouted. She hit him in the head, and his glasses flew off.

"Stop it, Cynthia!" I said loudly. "Hitting is not permitted."

I heard a knock at my door. Mona looked in. "Is everything okay?"

Cynthia burst into tears.

Her father reached for her. "Honey, I'm so sorry."

"Don't touch me!"

"Should I call security?" Mona asked me.

I shook my head, but I was perched on the edge of my seat, not knowing what to expect next. I knew I was

205

close to losing control of the session. In her pain, Cynthia seemed to be regressing, as though she were twelve years old again. I could tell Mona was concerned.

Cynthia glared at her father, even though the tears flowed freely. "How can you be sorry when you're still doing it? You're driving Mom crazy, and for what? She's going through menopause, and her body is going wacko on her. She gained thirty pounds. The woman is having mood swings and hot flashes, but instead of supporting her, you hound her night and day about her weight. That sucks! She's starving herself, just like I did when I was twelve years old!"

Mr. Reed reached for her again. She pushed him away again. "Besides, who are you to judge Mother, when you used to have a weight problem yourself?"

"That's precisely why I did it," he said. "Because I started putting on weight," he added. "Both of my parents had weight problems. My father died of a heart attack when he was only forty-two. My mother became diabetic." He paused and clasped his hands together and stared at them while his daughter cried.

"I was two years younger than my father when I had my heart attack," he said.

Cynthia snapped her head up. "What?"

Sudden tears filled his eyes. "That's right, Cynthia. You were ten years old at the time, and I was forty years old, forty pounds overweight, and smoking two packs of cigarettes a day. I was on the golf course when it happened."

"You never told me that!"

"I didn't tell anyone. Not even your mother."

Cynthia just looked at him, her mouth agape.

"It's true, honey. I didn't want to worry her. But it was a wake-up call for me." He wiped his eyes. "I was very scared for a long time. I guess I became irrational. A fanatic, like you said." He looked away, as if embarrassed.

Cynthia scooted closer and took his hand. "Oh, Daddy, I wish you had told us. All this time I thought you were ashamed of us. Of me," she added. "Every time I looked in the mirror, I saw a fat girl. A fat girl who never measured up. Why do you think I've had all these damned surgeries? I mean, just look at me!"

"Look at her lips," Mona mumbled. I shot her a glare. Fortunately Cynthia was trying to comfort her father and didn't seem to hear.

Cynthia's father looked at her. "Can you ever forgive me?"

They embraced. Cynthia looked up suddenly. "Are you okay now? I mean, is your heart okay?"

"Yes, sweetheart."

Mona sniffed and reached for a tissue and sat on the arm of the sofa. "This is so beautiful. I feel so lucky to have been a part of this."

I was touched as well.

"Please don't have any more surgery," Mr. Reed said to Cynthia.

"I promise," she said. "But we have to tell Mom the truth. We have to get things out in the open, Daddy."

"We'll tell her together, Cynthia."

"Doodlebug," she corrected with a tearful smile. "From now on, I want you to call me Doodlebug."

Mona and I slipped from the room, as though we both understood the two needed a moment alone.

"Boy, did I ever learn something today," Mona said.

"Yeah?" I looked at her.

"It's so easy to misunderstand other people's intentions, even those we're close to. We can't see inside their hearts, you know?"

I nodded and thought of my mother. If I had a dollar for each misunderstanding we'd ever had, I would be rich. I wouldn't be forced to take on patients like George Moss. But I'd never been able to get past the fake eyelashes and the heavy eye shadow and the mound of junk that surrounded her.

"I'm a terrible daughter," I said.

"Your mom isn't easy," Mona told me.

"I'm supposed to be this expert in relationships, but I've never been able to enjoy a close one with my own mother, and my marriage lasted all of three years. What does that tell you?"

"It isn't too late to fix things," Mona said.

After I closed the office and once I attended to Mike and her puppies, I drove to Little Five Points and parked behind my mother and aunt's new store. I found my mother at the stove in the kitchen. My mouth watered at the smells of her cooking. She wore a denim jumpsuit with matching eye shadow, and sported several over-sized rings that she'd obviously purchased at the local flea market. She looked surprised to see me.

"What's wrong?" she said.

"Nothing," I told her. "I just thought I'd drop by."

"Well, if you're here to see your Aunt Trixie, she's straightening up the studio."

"I'm here to see *you*, Mom."

She looked doubtful. "I hope you're here to tell me those mongrels are gone."

"Nope. They're still with me."

"Then it must be about your aunt Lou. She told me how you turned your back on her when she came to you pleading for help with her vaginal problems. I just want you to know I'm not getting in the middle of it."

"Mom?"

"I only have one piece of advice where your aunt Lou is concerned: try to steer clear of her for the next couple of weeks. At least until her itching eases up."

It suddenly occurred to me that, no matter how hard we tried, my mother and I would continue to rub each other wrong most of the time.

"I hope you're staying for dinner," she said after a moment. "I'm making my specialty, chicken-fried steak smothered with onions and gravy."

"That's my favorite!" I said. I saw her pleased smile.

She had always been a great cook. That went a long way toward making up for the touchy-feely relationship we lacked.

I arrived home feeling like a stuffed goose, after all I'd eaten. An anxious-looking Mike met me at the front door, but when I tried to let her outside, she wasn't interested. Instead, she went into the laundry room. I followed. I noted Runt lying by himself in the corner of the box. He was so tiny. I picked him up carefully, and my heart turned over in my chest at the cool, lifeless body.

Tears filled my eyes as I wrapped him in a towel. I wondered what to do with him. I put him on my washing machine and went to the phone. I called Jeff Henry's office and left a message. He returned my call immediately.

"One of the puppies is dead," I said, trying to swallow back my tears.

"The runt?" he asked gently.

"Yes."

"I'm sorry, Kate."

More tears. "I don't know what to do with him. If he were a goldfish, I'd know what to do, but he's not a goldfish. I don't know what to do."

"How far are you from my office?"

"Um." I tried to think. "Five or ten minutes," I finally said.

"Give me your address. I'll drive over and pick him up."

I didn't try to talk him out of it, even though I suspected it was an inconvenience and I would probably be charged for it. I gave him my address and returned to the laundry room, where I found Mike with her front paws pressed against the front of the washer, her nails clicking against the metal as she tried to reach her puppy.

"No, girl," I said and slipped my fingers inside her collar. I led her toward the box and convinced her to lie down, but I could tell she was anxious, even as her healthy puppies began to nurse. I sat on the floor and petted her. "I'm sorry," I said as fresh tears hit me. I kept petting her and telling her how sorry I was.

The doorbell rang, and I went to answer it. Jeff Henry stood on the other side, holding a small cardboard box. "Where's the pup?" he asked. I led him into the laundry room and pointed. I was so distraught, I didn't care that my kitchen looked like a demolition site. Jeff very gently put the little bundle in his box. Once again I had to coax Mike to her bed.

"I'll be right back," he said.

When he returned, I was sitting next to Mike's box, petting her and trying to soothe her. "I guess she knows what's going on," I told him. He sat on the floor as well.

"She'll be a little anxious for a while. How are you doing?"

I brushed tears from my cheeks. "I feel terrible about this. I shouldn't have gone out tonight. I should have stayed and made sure he ate. I should have asked you to teach me how to feed Runt with that tube you mentioned."

"I don't think it would have made a difference, Kate. Some puppies are born too small and too weak. You did what you could."

I nodded, but I couldn't stop crying. It was just one more loss I had to deal with. "You don't have to stay," I said. "Besides, I know the floor is uncomfortable. I just don't want to leave Mike."

"The floor doesn't bother me," he said. "I once had to crawl beneath an old car to help a Bluetick hound give birth. She bit me twice," he added with a chuckle. "I was nine years old at the time."

"You were obviously born to do this kind of work."

"I grew up on a farm. I discovered at an early age that I got along better with animals than people."

That surprised me, because he seemed so personable, and he was stylishly dressed, his beige linen slacks and powder blue oxford shirt neatly pressed. His brown hair was neat, his face made more handsome by his tendency to smile easily.

We both stroked Mike's head and talked softly. Mike finally settled down and went to sleep. Jeff moved beside me, and we leaned against the wall. "Thank you for coming," I said. "I didn't know I would take it so hard."

He took my hand and squeezed it. "It bothers me, too," he said, "and I do this sort of thing for a living. But the little fellow is in puppy heaven now," he added, "so you don't have to worry about him anymore."

I looked at him. "You really think there's a heaven for dogs?"

"Of course," he said. "Animals give so much love. What would a heaven be without them?"

I could certainly see Runt admitted into heaven more quickly than somebody like Bitsy Stout, who could quote scripture word for word but did her best to make people miserable.

"I'm going through some crummy stuff in my personal life right now," I said. "I guess that's one reason I'm so upset about Runt."

"I'm sorry you're having a tough go of it. I'm a good listener."

I hesitated. "I'm going to be divorced Friday at eleven a.m."

"Oh, boy, that's a tough one. You and your husband can't work things out?"

I shrugged. "We've tried. But the arguments are always the same. Like playing a broken record, but the grooves are pretty worn out and the music is scratchy."

"That's a unique way to put it."

"Have you ever been married?"

"No. I don't think it's in the cards for me."

Again, I was surprised, and I wondered if he'd suffered a broken heart as well. But he didn't elaborate, and I didn't push. He told me about vet school and setting up his practice. He asked me about my own practice, having read on his office form that I was a psychologist. At some point I must've dozed because, when I opened my eyes, I was mortified to find my head on his shoulder.

"It's okay," he said. "I think I drifted off for a few

minutes myself." He checked his wristwatch. "It's after midnight. I should get home. Are you feeling better?"

"Yes." I noticed Mike was calm as well. She remained still, even as her pups nursed greedily.

I was yawning as I led Jeff to the front door. He took my hand for the second time that evening and squeezed it. "I'll call you tomorrow and see how Mike and her kiddos are doing," he said. "Try to get some sleep."

I thanked him and watched him walk to his car. Despite being sad over losing Runt, I had enjoyed spending time with Jeff. He was easy to talk to, and it was obvious he cared about his little patients. As he pulled from my drive, I wondered if it was his custom to make house calls. I was almost certain he wasn't accustomed to sitting on a woman's laundry room floor while she cried and then fell asleep with her head on his shoulder. I wondered if I was developing a small crush on the handsome veterinarian.

Or, maybe, I was just hoping there was still something left of my heart after its having been so thoroughly shattered.

The next morning, as I waited for Jack and Martha Hix to arrive for their weekly couples counseling session, I told Mona about losing Runt and spending part of the evening with Dr. Henry. "I need to call Mrs. Perez and let her know," I said.

"I'm sorry you lost the puppy," Mona said, "but I

know you and Mrs. Perez worked hard to keep the little fellow going." She smiled. "One good thing that came out of it was meeting Dr. Henry. You like him, don't you?"

"I can't help but like him."

"No, I mean, you *really* like him. Like him as in wanting to see what's under his white lab coat."

"Sorry to disappoint you, Mona, but I haven't even thought of it. He's just a very nice man who happens to be good-looking as well."

"I guess it's hard to think of a man in that light when you're still in love with your husband, huh?" she said. "Friday will be here before you know it."

We exchanged looks. The sudden lump in my throat that always showed up when I thought about Jay, along with the loss of Runt, kept me from answering at first. "I used to think love was enough, Mona," I said. "I used to think if two people loved each other, they could get through anything. But that's not the way it is in real life."

Mona just looked at me. "That is the saddest thing I've ever heard you say," she said.

"Sorry."

She shrugged. "But it brings us back to what we were discussing," she said. "If your marriage is over, maybe it's *time* to start thinking about what the cute Dr. Henry looks like under his lab coat."

chapter 15

·····························

I saw the crowd in front of my house as I turned onto my street; at least two dozen people were carrying large signs that read WIPE OUT PORNOGRAPHY. I felt like turning around and driving in the opposite direction. Damn that Bitsy Stout; she insisted on making my life miserable.

As I drove closer, I saw her leading the group. Several of my neighbors watched from lawn chairs in their front yards, and cars were parked along the street, passengers staring from the windows. I muttered a four-letter word when I spied a white van bearing the name of our local news station and a reporter talking into a camera.

Just a typical day in my screwed-up life, I thought.

I pulled into my driveway, only to be rushed by the reporter, who banged on my window. I rolled it down.

"Are you Kate Holly?" he asked.

The news camera was directed right at me. "I'm Dr. Holly," I said, sounding as professional as I could under the circumstances. "May I help you?"

"Are you aware that you have a pornographic statue in your flower bed?"

"I have a statue, but I assure you there is nothing pornographic about it. Actually, it's a religious piece created by my mother and my aunt, who are artists. Would you please step back so I can get out of my car?"

The reporter did as I asked, even though the cameraman continued to film. Once I climbed from my car, the reporter wasted no time grilling me. I was thankful I was wearing my best black-and-white pinstriped suit.

"We understand the entire congregation from a local church is demanding that you remove the statue," he said.

"Yes," I said squarely into the camera. "Not only have some of the members trespassed onto my property, they've defaced it and made threatening phone calls to my office." I had to pause to catch my breath. "I think your viewers would be better served if you investigated the validity of the so-called church." I smiled pleasantly. I'll have to admit that even I was impressed with my handling of the situation. "Now, if you'll excuse me, I have to call my attorney."

The reporter looked into the camera, his eyes gleaming with excitement as he gave an overview to those just tuning in. It amazed me that Bitsy Stout and her nutso church group had managed to get live coverage. It wasn't as though Atlanta lacked for news.

I held my head high and walked calmly to my front door, but I was so mad I felt I could have torn it open with my teeth. I could tell Bitsy was having the time of her life parading about with her buddies. I wondered which of the men in her group had threatened me.

I heard Mike barking from inside as I unlocked my door. I had to grab her collar to keep her from darting out when she caught sight of all the people. I let her out the back door and called Mona.

"I need a lawyer," I said and gave her a quick run-down of what was happening.

"I hope you were holding in your stomach," Mona said. "I hear TV makes you look ten pounds heavier."

As always, Mona had her priorities in order, but at the moment I was too angry to care what my stomach looked like on TV. "I don't even like that statue," I said. "I'd dig it up myself if I weren't afraid I'd hurt Mom and Trixie's feelings."

"I don't remember seeing it," Mona said.

"You've seen my living room, if that tells you any-thing. I'm surprised they haven't stuck pink flamingos in my yard as well."

"Poor Kate," she said. "You might have to move into a trailer park so you'll blend. I'll call my attorney right away."

I checked on the puppies and felt a stab of sorrow in my heart that Runt was no longer among them. I tried to imagine him playing and tumbling about with other puppies in doggie heaven. Mrs. Perez had been sorry to hear that Runt hadn't made it, but she was convinced he was in a better place. She'd watched a TV psychic tell a woman that her deceased mother, as well as her mother's beloved but long-deceased shih tzu, were together in the afterlife.

I was surprised to discover that Jeff Henry had called, as promised, to make sure I was okay and to remind me to contact him, night or day, if I needed him. I knew Mona would read more into it, but I told myself I'd lucked out and found a really nice vet. In all honesty, I wasn't sure I would recognize the difference between a man who was simply being nice to me and one who was showing interest.

I let Mike in, gave her a treat, and freshened her food and water. I could tell she was antsy over the sounds coming from my front yard. "I should have told you about my crazy neighbor before you moved in," I said. "In the meantime, you're going to have to stay in your room." I put her in the laundry room and closed the door.

Mona called back from her cell phone. "I'm on my way over," she said. "My attorney advised you to call the police. Bitsy and her church people have no legal right to picket without a permit, and if they set one foot in your yard, they're trespassing."

"Of course they're trespassing," I said, peeking out my living room window. "They're all over my front yard. Fortunately the news van is gone. Damn, I hate getting the police involved. Especially since they have it on record that I threatened Bitsy and gave her the finger," I added.

"What are you going to do?"

"Ignore them. That will spoil Bitsy's fun, because she hates being ignored."

"I have an idea," Mona said. "It might just solve your problems. I'll see you shortly."

I went upstairs to change. I was hungry, but I didn't feel like cooking. My doorbell rang, and I hurried to let Mona in. Instead I found my mother and Aunt Trixie standing on the other side.

"We saw you on TV," my mother said. "Where's that dog of yours?"

"I put her in the laundry room," I said and stepped back to let them in.

"You looked really nice talking to that newsman," my aunt said, "and you came across so well."

"Did I look fat?"

"Oh, no," she said.

"You could have improved your posture," my mother said, "but I'm probably the only one who noticed."

I looked at her. "You think?"

My mother stood at the window, peering through the curtains. "Just so you know, I gave Bitsy a piece of my mind," she said. "I told her she and her church group were nothing but a bunch of crazy Holy Rollers."

"What did she say?"

"She said God was on their side."

· What Looks Like Crazy ·

"Oh, great," I said. "I'll probably be swarmed by locusts." I barely got the words out of my mouth before I heard a couple of loud thunks outside my door.

"You are *not* going to believe what they're doing!" my mother all but shouted. "That idiot woman is throwing rocks at the statue. That's it! I'm going out there to kick some butt!"

"No!" I said, racing toward the door and flattening myself against it to block her. My mother tried to get past me, and we did a little dance. "You are *not* going out there!" I looked at my aunt. "Call nine-one-one." I figured it would be easier facing the cops than pulling my mother off Bitsy.

Mona and the police pulled up within seconds of each other. I gave my mother a stern look. "I'm going outside to take care of this, and I except you to stay put," I said. "If you start any trouble, you can forget grandchildren."

My mother shrank back.

Outside, most of Bitsy's followers were scattering; the sight of the police car had obviously scared them away. Bitsy stood her ground, but I could see her resolve and bravery fading as I listed my complaints.

The officers looked at Bitsy. "Is this true?" one of them asked her.

She squirmed. "Yes. But I don't know anything about threatening phone calls. I think she's making it up."

The officer turned to me. "Do you wish to press charges against Miss Stout?"

I looked at Bitsy. "It depends."

"I won't do it again," Bitsy promised. "I'll stop being a pesky neighbor."

"Not good enough," I said. "I want your sour cream coffee cake recipe." She gasped and clutched her heart. "You have twenty-four hours to hand it over. I want every single ingredient listed, and I want it printed out neatly so I can read it."

Her eyes hardened. "I hope you know you're going to hell."

I smiled. "The question is, do *you* want to go to jail?"

A black Mercedes pulled into my driveway as Bitsy stalked from my yard and the police drove away. My mother and aunt joined me. A well-dressed man approached. "Am I to understand you are the owner of that stunning sculpture I saw on TV?" he asked in an English accent.

"Yes," I said. "Who are you?"

He handed me his card. "I'm the curator of our art museum, and I would love to have that piece as part of our religious art. I'm willing to pay handsomely for it."

My mother's and Trixie's mouths dropped open at the same time. I glanced at Mona, who winked. I knew Mona's late husband had supported the arts when he'd been alive. "Gee, I don't know," I said. "It was a gift from my beloved mother and aunt. I couldn't possibly part with it."

My mother yanked me aside. "Are you crazy?" she hissed. "Think of the money. Think what it will mean for

Trixie and me to have one of our sculptures in the High Museum of Art! Trixie and I will make you another one just like it. It's only junk," she added with a hiss.

"No, Mom," I said firmly. "I don't want a replacement. There are some things in this world that are simply irreplaceable."

"Okay, whatever it takes," she said.

I turned to the curator. "This is one of the hardest decisions I've ever made, but the statue is yours. But I can't, in good conscience, accept money. I would like to donate it to the museum."

"You are too kind," the curator said.

"It'll probably take a jackhammer to get it out of the ground."

"Not to worry," the man said, shaking my hand to firm up the deal. He winked.

An hour later, my mother and Aunt Trixie were sitting across the table from Mona and me at a nearby pizza parlor. We'd ordered beer to celebrate the fact that the Junk Sisters would have their work on display at the art museum.

"You should have taken the money," my mother said. "I caught a look at your kitchen. It needs serious work."

"Actually, I'm in the process of redecorating," I told her.

We had almost finished eating our pizza when Jeff Henry walked through the door, followed by another man close to his age. They stepped up to the counter and began studying the menu.

I nudged Mona. "It's the vet," I whispered.

"That's Dr. Henry?" she said, her eyes combing him appreciatively. "Nice. Who's the good-looking guy beside him?"

I shrugged. "I have no idea."

"You should call him over."

I was just about to wave to him when the man standing beside Jeff at the counter reached over and stroked his hand lightly. The two shared a private look, then inched apart as a young girl stepped behind the register to take their order.

Mona and I exchanged looks. "Maybe you shouldn't call him over after all," she said.

I excused myself and headed for the ladies' room, where I decided to hide out. Mona joined me a few minutes later. "They're gone. They just picked up a to-go order. Your mother asked me to check on you."

"I feel like an idiot," I said. "I thought he liked me."

"I'd say he liked you very much, to sit in your laundry room with you half the night after you lost Runt. I'd say you have a nice new friend who just happens to be a great vet. And who doesn't need more friends?"

I didn't respond.

"Besides, you're not *really* interested in a new relationship," she said. "You're still in love with your husband. If you can't see that, then, yes, you're an idiot." She opened the bathroom door and motioned me out. "After you."

Mona drove me home, and the sisters headed back to

Little Five Points. "We need to finalize plans for the mental health fair," Mona said as she drove. "It's this Friday."

"You want to discuss it *now*?" I asked. The mere thought made me want to bail out of the car even though we were traveling at fifty miles per hour. I sighed. "Just tell me what I need to do," I said with dread in my voice.

"You'll need to mingle with reporters."

I looked at her. "Reporters?"

"I've sent out press releases, so you should have plenty of coverage. You'll want to act real compassionate. Also, it will give you a chance to discuss the importance of good mental health. Oh, and don't forget to mention our open house the first Monday of each month."

Mona dropped me off at my house. After letting Mike out, I decided to take a drive. Driving helped me think, and I had a lot to think about. And the truth was, I felt lonely.

I needed to talk to somebody, and the person I wanted to talk to was Jay. But I couldn't talk to Jay, because I was divorcing him. It wasn't fair to call him and give him mixed messages. It wasn't healthy for me to listen to his voice, because every time I heard it, my heart got sucked in.

I felt desperate. That's the only excuse I could think of for ending up at Thad's house. Fortunately his was the only car in the driveway, so I assumed he was alone. When he didn't answer the door, I walked around back and peeked over his fence. I wasn't surprised to find him in his hot tub, leaning back with a towel propped beneath his head, a frozen margarita in one hand. I opened the gate, and Thad looked up.

"Kate, what a surprise! Take off your clothes and hop in. I'm celebrating."

"Close your eyes."

"Like I don't know how you look naked?"

I waited. Finally he closed his eyes. I stripped down to my panties and climbed into the tub, taking care not to get my cast wet. "Oh, boy, this feels great," I said. "What are you celebrating?"

"My little brother has moved on with his life. He doesn't need me around anymore."

"Of course he needs you," I said. "You're his brother. You're family. Family is important."

"Here, have a drink," Thad said. "Your thinking is skewed at the moment. If families were so great, there wouldn't be such a crucial need for family therapists."

"True," I said with a shrug. I took a sip and closed my eyes. I'd forgotten how good Thad's margaritas were. He added a little orange juice to his recipe so that it went down more smoothly. The salt along the rim tasted good on my tongue. "This is delicious."

Thad scooted closer. "Just like old times, huh?"

"Sort of." I offered him the glass, but he shook his head. "You look like you need it more than I do. Bad day?"

"I keep hoping my life will become sane again."

"You take life too seriously, Kate."

"Maybe I need a hot tub."

"All you need is a close personal friend with a hot tub."

"Good idea. You just saved me about five thousand dollars."

He was silent for a moment, as though sensing that I needed the quiet, that I needed to unwind.

"Remember Cancún?" he said after a moment. "We should go back."

Beneath the bubbling water, I felt Thad rub one hairy leg against mine.

"Just imagine, Kate," he said, his voice lulling me. "White beaches, crystal clear water, leisurely naps beneath a ceiling fan." He smiled. "And room service. You know how much you love room service."

"Room service," I said dreamily, letting my mind drift in that direction. I would not have to eat frozen dinners that tasted like cardboard. People would deliver exotic foods on trays covered with crisp, white cloths, and nice china. As I sipped my drink, I could almost smell the suntan oil.

"You are in dire need of pampering," Thad said, refilling my glass from the pitcher. "And I'm the perfect man for the job. Losing you humbled me, Kate."

I gave him a look.

"Okay, 'humble' is a strong word, but it made me think," he said. "I should have treated you better."

"Yep."

"But try to see it from my side. It has always been too easy for me where women are concerned. I've never had to go out of my way like I did with you. Women were just happy to be with me, you know?"

"So you're saying it wasn't really your fault that you were a two-timing jerk?"

He sighed. "I cheated *once*, Kate. And it was sort of an accident."

"No, Thad. Backing your car into the mailbox is an accident. Stubbing your toe on the leg of a chair is an accident. Getting naked with your receptionist in your hot tub requires thought and planning."

He took the glass and sipped before handing it back to me. "Okay, the truth is, I did you a favor," he said.

"Excuse me?"

"I knew you were slipping away from me. But I also know you can't stand the thought of hurting somebody. I made it easy for you to get out."

I stared at him, openmouthed. "Are you saying you set the whole thing up on my account? That you *intended* for me to catch you in the hot tub with another woman so that I'd have an easier time breaking up with you?"

"My actions weren't completely altruistic," he admitted. "I wasn't about to tell my friends you'd broken it off because you were bored with me. I mean, I have a certain reputation to live up to, you know?"

"I don't believe what I'm hearing! You *used* a human being, a woman, so that I would break up with you in a way that would make you look like a stud to your buddies?"

"See, there you go making it sound like I did a bad thing."

"Jeez, Thad!"

"My receptionist had been giving me the come-on for months. She came here that night uninvited. When it all comes down to it, I was the true victim."

"Give me a break!"

"Well, look what you did! You married the first guy to come along. I guess you really showed me, huh?"

"You think I married Jay to punish you?"

"Well, didn't you?"

"No, Thad." I saw the look of amazement in his eyes. "It had nothing to do with you."

"Now, Kate—"

"I married Jay because I loved him."

"Oh." He leaned back in the tub and seemed to consider it. "So why are you getting divorced?"

"Because Jay's job is dangerous, and I have no desire to be a young widow."

"You shouldn't have to be. That's why I'm even more convinced we should fly to Cancún. You and I were pretty darn good together, Kate. I've learned my lesson."

I decided not to answer. I didn't want to burst Thad's ego bubble by telling him there was a difference between good and fantastic. I did not want to be the one to break it to him that there was more to a relationship than sharing a bed. I knew what it was like to share souls.

229

I jumped when I felt Thad's hand on my thigh. "Don't give me your answer now," he said. "Let me go in and make a fresh pitcher of margaritas."

I averted my gaze as he climbed from the tub. "I should go. I think I'm getting drunk."

"No, you just stay put. You can always stay here if you can't drive. I'll make us a little snack." He turned for the door, paused, then turned back with a grin and snatched up my clothes.

"What are you doing?" I asked.

"Just making sure you don't try to sneak off on me," he said.

"Don't take my clothes!" I said, but it was too late. I caught sight of Thad's behind as he hurried toward the glass doors leading inside.

"Dammit!" I climbed awkwardly from the hot tub, with the full use of only one hand, and started for the door—then realized I would be asking for big trouble. I knew Thad's game only too well. Also, I was feeling the effects of the margarita. God only knew how much tequila was coursing through my bloodstream. The only thing I *did* know was that I had to get out of there fast. I spied a large towel and wrapped it around me sarong-style. Then I grabbed my purse and high heels and ran for my car.

chapter 16

······························

I grabbed the door handle, then paused. I had enough of a buzz going that I didn't trust myself to drive. Fortunately I had my cell phone and could call Mona. I whipped it out, started to dial, then reconsidered.

Did I really want Mona to know that I had been desperate enough to climb in Thad's hot tub? Wasn't it bad enough that she knew I'd had a semicrush on a gay guy? I heard Thad calling me, and I jumped behind his hedges and crouched on the ground. Luckily it was dark, and Thad would probably never think to look for me in his bushes. It bothered me that this was the second time in two weeks I'd found myself in such a predicament. It was times like these that made me question whether I was really capable of treating people for psychological disorders.

Finally Thad grew quiet. I checked Information for the number of a local cab company and dialed. The cab arrived twenty minutes later. I raced across Thad's front yard and opened the back door to the cab. "I'm sort of in a hurry," I said, then rattled off my address. The driver glanced back at me. I recognized Tony.

He frowned. "Don't I know you?"

"I almost never take cabs."

"The lady in the black dress," he said, as though a lightbulb had suddenly flashed on in his head. "Nice towel. What happened to your wrist?"

"I fell. Like I said, I'm in a hurry."

He drove on. "When did you start working this neighborhood?"

"I could ask you the same thing," I said.

"I'm filling in for a guy who's getting married. Maybe it's time you think about settling down. This is no kind of life for a pretty girl like yourself."

"I'm not a hooker, okay? I'm just a person who makes dumb choices. Could you drive a little faster?"

I was thankful it was dark when I arrived home. "Would you cut your headlights, please," I asked Tony as I counted out my money. If Bitsy saw me arrive home in a towel, she would think I was a sinner of the worst kind and renege on giving me her coffee cake recipe. "Could you pick me up in the morning? I need to go back and get my car. Eight a.m.?"

He nodded. "You should let me introduce you to my nephew, Tony. He's looking for a wife."

"I'm not interested in meeting anyone right now, but thanks. I'll see you tomorrow morning, eight sharp." I climbed from the cab and skulked toward my house. Mike greeted me as I stepped inside. The good thing about Mike is that I can walk in wearing a towel, and I don't have to try to explain it.

The phone rang as I let her out. I saw Thad's name on my caller ID and ignored it. He didn't leave a message. Jay had called. I played his message back.

"Saw you on the six o'clock news," he said. "All the guys in the station said you looked hot."

I grabbed a shower, slathered myself with my Donna Karan lotion, and sprayed the perfume on my neck. I reached for my favorite sleep shirt, then remembered the Jones New York pajamas that Mona had surprised me with some months back. Because the set was so exquisite, I had hung it in my closet and seldom wore it for fear of spilling Ben & Jerry's chocolate ice cream on it. The material felt so good on my skin that I promised myself to wear this set more often. It was crazy to keep it in my closet when it gave me such a luxurious feeling.

I slipped between my sheets, turned off my lamp, and put the day behind me, where it belonged. I visualized a sandy white beach, the sun warming my body, seagulls flying overhead, and a vast ocean. I smelled the briny air, heard waves crashing, and at last I felt my body relax.

Thad was right; I *did* need pampering. But I didn't have to go all the way to Cancún to get it.

My doorbell rang the next morning at precisely eight a.m. Tony stood on the other side of the door; next to him was a younger man who had Tony's dark looks but was about fifty pounds overweight.

"This is the nephew I was telling you about," Tony said. "His name is Tony, too. Half the people in our family are named Tony."

"Very nice to meet you," I said, shaking the nephew's hand. I looked at the older Tony. "I'm in a huge hurry."

"That's the problem with you young people," he said. "You're always in a big rush. One day the whole lot of you will be old, and you'll wonder where the time went."

"You're right," I said, and saw the surprised look on his face. "Thank you for reminding me."

Tony-the-nephew tried to strike up a conversation with me before we pulled from my driveway. In an attempt to discourage him, I pulled my cell phone from my purse and called my mother.

"What's wrong?" she asked quickly.

"Nothing," I said. "I thought I'd check in, see how you're doing."

"Why?"

"I didn't realize I needed a reason."

The younger Tony shrugged and turned around in his seat.

"I hate to be the bearer of bad news, but your aunt Lou is still upset with you."

I knew my mother was lying. She loved giving bad news. "I'm sorry to hear it," I said, "but it doesn't change the fact that I can't write prescriptions for her."

"Uncle Bump is hurt, seeing as how he tried so hard to be a father figure to you."

I said nothing.

"Lucien isn't very happy either," she said. "It's sad that you don't have a relationship with your only cousin."

"Have you *looked* at Lucien lately?" I asked. "The guy is scary. He's scarier than some of my patients."

"Your aunt Lou raised him. What can you expect?"

She had a point. But at least Lucien had not been forced to get up before dawn every Saturday and comb the streets of Buckhead in a beat-up pickup truck before the garbagemen arrived, just to see what the wealthy were tossing out.

"I've got to go, Mom," I said, determined not to let her ruin my day. I leaned my head back against the seat and closed my eyes. Fortunately the men in front seemed to get the message. They were quiet the rest of the way. I was relieved to find Thad's car gone when we pulled into his driveway. I paid the fare. As I was getting out of the cab, the younger Tony looked at me.

"You want to give me your phone number so I can call you?" he asked.

I gave him my best smile. "This isn't a good time for me, but thanks for asking." I hurried to my car.

I made it to my office in record time and was stunned to find Harold Fry in my reception room. "Oh, thank goodness you're okay!" I said. But my relief was short-lived. I glanced at Mona, who was pacing the room, eyes blazing like something you might see in a scary demonic movie.

"What's wrong?" I asked.

"You will *not* believe what Agent Fry has discovered!" she said. "Dr. Manning, the chiropractor, is a fraud!"

"You mean he's not really a chiropractor?"

"Right," Harold said. "Even worse, he preys on women who are well-off and vulnerable. He insists on taking a ton of X-rays, and he has the patients come in several times a week, which they do because—"

"Because he's a creep," Mona cut in. "He pretends to be attracted to them so they can't wait for their next appointment."

Harold nodded. "*And*, because he doesn't know what he's doing, he usually ends up causing more damage."

"Which explains why I've been in so much pain," Mona said. "And it gets worse. He's married with three kids!"

"How do you know all this?" I asked Harold.

"Last time he was here, I asked him to look into it," Mona said. "I didn't tell you because I thought you'd get mad."

"The name 'Dan Manning' is an alias," Harold said. "He was forced to close his Virginia office because patients began complaining. He packed up in the middle of the night and took off."

"Good thing I asked Agent Fry to check him out, huh?" Mona said. "I've already contacted my attorney."

I was almost certain the American Psychological Association could put my license through a shredder over something like this. I tried to think what other skills I had to fall back on so that I wouldn't end up homeless. Nothing came to mind. I would probably end up collecting junk with my mother and aunt. As a junior member of their corporation, I would be the one sent down into the Dumpsters.

"Do me a favor," I said to Mona. "Kevin Bosley is due in shortly—"

"We're not going to have to go back up on the roof, are we?" she asked.

I ignored the remark. "Would you try to reach him and see if he can reschedule for later today?"

"Sure." She began searching through her Rolodex.

"Harold, I'd like to see you in my office," I told him. He followed me inside, and I closed the door. I motioned to the sofa. "You've been very busy," I said, taking a seat on my chair.

"Yeah. To tell you the truth, I'm kind of tired and feeling out of sorts."

He looked tired. The opposite of a manic high is often depression. It wouldn't be long before Harold crashed. My job was to get him through it. "Are you taking your medication?" I already knew the answer.

"I can't take medication when I'm on a job," he said. "It clouds my judgment."

"Well, it sounds like you've solved the case, so this might be a good time to get back on track." I would wait until Harold was stable before I lowered the boom on him, but I was not going to continue seeing him until we came to an understanding about his meds. "What do you think about calling your sister to come stay with you for a while?" I asked.

"I'll make a deal," Harold said. "I'll call my sister and get back on my medication, but you have to promise not to blow my cover where Mona is concerned."

"Blow your cover?" I asked.

"Meaning I don't want her to know that I'm just a retired tax accountant. Let her keep thinking I'm CIA." He smiled. "I think it turns her on."

I had just finished up with Harold when Mona peeked in my door. "Alice Smithers is on line two. She's crying. Do you think she just realized what bad taste she has?"

I picked up the phone. "What's wrong, Alice?" I asked quickly.

"Liz's boyfriend is in my condo," she whispered. "I opened the door to leave for work, and he shoved me back inside. He was really drunk."

"Did he hurt you?"

More tears. "He beat me up pretty bad. I grabbed my cell phone and locked myself in the bathroom. He seems to have passed out on the sofa, but I'm afraid he'll wake up if I try to get past him to the front door."

"You've called the police, right?"

"He'll kill me if I report him," she hissed.

"He'll kill you if you don't!" I said, noting that I had Mona's undivided attention.

"I'm so scared, Kate. I'm so scared."

I blinked several times at the change in her voice. She suddenly sounded childlike.

"Give me your address," I said, not wanting to take the time to look it up. When she didn't respond, I became insistent. "Alice, talk to me!"

"I can't remember it."

"You don't remember your address?" I wondered whether Alice had a head injury. I was vaguely aware of Mona racing from my office. Suddenly there was a crashing sound from the other end of the line, followed by a booming male voice. Alice cried out.

I jumped to my feet. "Alice, get out of the apartment!" I shouted. Her phone went dead. "Dammit!" I cried.

"I've got her address, and I'm dialing nine-one-one now," Mona called out from the next room.

It was all I could do to focus on Kevin Bosley's words as I waited for word on Alice. This was only my second session with Kevin after his attempt to hurl himself off the roof, so I wanted it to go well.

A complete physical by his family doctor confirmed that he was in excellent physical condition; and since Kevin had no history of depression, nor was his family tree saddled with it, I felt it was situational. I was not going to delve too deeply into his psyche until I was certain he was stable.

"How's the depression?" I asked.

"Well, I don't feel like jumping off rooftops."

"That's a good sign," I said, giving him a thumbs-up. "How are you sleeping?"

"Better. I decided to hold off interviewing for a new job until I get through this, so that lowered my stress level."

"That is an excellent idea," I said, delighted he'd thought of it himself. "Are you getting out of the house?" Depressed people tend to isolate, which is the worst thing they can do.

"I've been walking the mall, and I've seen a lot of movies."

"What about hobbies?"

"I used to play tennis. I'm pretty good. Also, I biked with these guys. I've got a fifteen-hundred-dollar bicycle in my garage collecting dust."

"I'd say it's about time you dust off that bicycle."

Kevin smiled for the first time since I'd met him.

"Have you heard anything about Alice?" I asked Mona once I'd scheduled Kevin's next appointment and walked him out.

"Nobody will tell me anything," she said.

I knew somebody who could get me the information I wanted. I called Jay and explained the situation.

"I'll see what I can find out," he said.

Mona and I waited. She practically dove on the phone each time it rang. Finally she handed me the receiver. "It's Jay."

"Here's what I've got so far," he said. "The cops arrived at the scene and found a badly beaten woman. There was nobody else inside the condo. The woman was taken by ambulance to the ER." He gave me the name of the hospital.

"Thank you, Jay," I said.

"Anytime, Katie."

I hung up the phone and passed the news on to Mona. "Would you please cancel my appointments for the rest of the day? I'm going to go to the hospital."

She nodded. "I know this is bad timing, but Mrs. Perez is picking me up shortly to take me to the chiropractor her cousin uses. Maybe he can undo some of the damage that jerk upstairs did to me."

"What's going to happen to Dr. Manning?"

"My lawyer has already contacted the police; there is a detective looking into it. It's all hush-hush since they don't want him to suspect anything and take off again. Speaking of jerks, George Moss called. He thinks you should give him another chance. I told him to forget it."

"Don't worry about coming back to the office today," I told her.

"Nancy won't be around to help with the phones," Mona said. "She has several job interviews set up today."

"Let the answering machine pick up the calls. I'll be back later to check it."

"You'll have to meet with Omar when he comes in," Mona said.

"Omar? Is he a new patient?"

"He's performing at the mental health fair, but he has to be paid up front." She handed me an envelope with his name on it.

I could have argued with Mona about spending money on an event that made no sense to me, but I would have been wasting my breath. Besides, it was her money. "Omar the Great, huh?" I said. "What's so great about him?"

"He's a famous sword swallower."

"Well, that's something you don't see every day."

"His brother, Gus the Great, was supposed to perform, but he discovered he was overbooked."

"Is Gus a sword swallower too?" I asked.

Mona shook her head. "He's a knife thrower."

"Oh, well, that makes sense," I lied. Nothing seemed to make sense in my life these days.

I drove to the hospital, parked as close to the emergency entrance as I could, and hurried inside. The waiting area was crowded and noisy. The receptionist informed me they did not have a patient by the name of Alice Smithers.

"There must be some mistake," I said. "I was told she was brought here by ambulance."

The woman called the nurses' station. "I'm sorry," she said. "Nobody named Smithers."

I stepped aside so that the person in line behind me could approach the desk. I wondered whether Jay had been given the wrong hospital, but knowing the vicinity where Alice lived, I felt certain I was in the right place.

I took a seat in one of the chairs and wondered what to do next. Something didn't feel right. I tried to think what it might be. For one thing, it made no sense that Liz Jones was gone, but her boyfriend was still coming around. What made him think he could just barge in on Alice? Had he been so drunk that he hadn't been thinking straight? If he and Liz had this hot thing going, why wasn't he with her? Why hadn't Liz returned for her clothes?

So many unanswered questions.

I recalled how terrified Alice had sounded, so terrified that she couldn't give me her address. I would not have even recognized her voice had I not known it was Alice calling to begin with.

I was missing something. I ran through my list of possibilities. Alice had a serious problem with boundaries. Her mother was an alcoholic. I knew in my gut there had been some form of abuse. That Alice was unable to forgive the abuse suggested it was bad. Children of abuse felt trapped and terrified. They feared telling on the abuser, so they had to find ways to cope.

I suddenly had a chilling thought. I knew one way they coped.

I returned to the receptionist's desk. "Would you please check and see if you have a patient by the name of Liz Jones?"

chapter 17

•••••••••••••••••••••••••••••

"I'm fairly certain Alice Smithers has dissociative phenomena," I told Thad as we sipped coffee in the hospital cafeteria and waited for her to get out of X-ray. The attending physician was checking for head trauma. I had called Thad and asked him to meet me at the hospital. Without going into details, I had told him it was urgent. Thankfully, he'd gotten over my slipping out on him, and he had driven straight over. He had listened quietly as I'd tried to back up my reasoning.

"Well, multiples are pretty rare," he said, "but it would explain what's going on with this patient. I wouldn't mind taking a look."

"That's why I called you. I want your opinion."

He stirred his coffee. "Oh, so this wasn't just an excuse to see me again?"

I chuckled. "I don't know what I'm going to do with you."

"The question is, what would you do *without* me?"

I had to admit it was a valid question. We finished our coffee and headed for the elevators. Thad punched the button, and we waited until the elevator cleared before we stepped on. I gave scant notice to the uniformed man standing before the control panel.

"What floor?" he asked.

I knew that voice. I turned. "Mr. Lewey!"

He gave me a sheepish smile. "Hey, Dr. Kate," he said. "How's the wrist?"

"What are *you* doing here? And why are you wearing that uniform and operating an elevator? You don't like elevators."

"I felt so bad over what happened the last time I saw you, especially after Mona convinced me I was a creep, that I decided to take action and finally *do* something about my problem. Instead of expecting you to fix everything for me," he added.

I noted he was holding the door open so that others could get on. "I'm so proud of you! Would you please take me to the first floor?"

"You got it, Dr. Kate."

Thad and I exited the elevator a moment later and headed for the ER. All he had to do was smile at the receptionist, and she pushed a buzzer that opened the metal doors leading to the treatment area.

The policeman standing outside Alice's door stepped aside when I told him that Thad and I were doctors and needed to consult with my patient. I paused before going in.

"Has the man responsible for her injuries been located?" I asked.

"Still looking," he said.

Thad and I walked into the room. The woman inside was badly beaten, and was wearing a short leather skirt, a tight blouse, and red Prada high heels. She was groggy and complaining to the nurse for not allowing her to smoke. She looked at me. I could barely pick out Alice's features beneath the heavy makeup and bruises.

"Well, well, look at what the wind blew in," she said derisively. Her voice sounded nothing like Alice's. She turned her attention to Thad, and her eyes took him in hungrily. "I hope you're my doctor, because the other guy isn't much to look at, if you get my meaning." She gave him a come-hither smile, then winced and touched her swollen lips.

"You're going to have to lie still, hon," the nurse said. "You've got a couple of cracked ribs." The nurse gave us a curious look as she left the exam room.

I stepped closer to the bed. I did not want to call Liz by name. "This is an associate of mine," I said, motioning to Thad. "Dr. Glazer. He's a psychiatrist. I'd like your permission to have him present while I speak with you."

She shrugged.

Thad offered his hand. "And you are?"

"Liz Jones." She glanced at me briefly as they shook hands. "You'll have to excuse my appearance," she said. "My prick ex-boyfriend got drunk and beat the crap out of me. The cops are waiting to take my statement. I'm going to have his ass thrown in jail this time."

"Has the doctor said whether you've suffered any head trauma?" I asked.

"My head is fine," she said, her words clipped, "but he wants to keep me overnight for observation, which sucks, since I can't smoke."

"I'd like to see you in my office as soon as possible," I said.

She looked smug. "I'll bet you would. But that's not going to happen, if I have any say in the matter."

"What makes you say that?" Thad asked.

She didn't look at him; her gaze was still fixed on me. "Because it's a waste of time," she said. "I know what she wants."

"Perhaps you'll reconsider," Thad said. "Dr. Holly and I share a genuine interest in getting to know you better." He gave her his card. "In the meantime, please call me if you need anything."

"Sure." She studied the card before tucking it inside her bra.

Thad and I left the room a few minutes later. "The person we just spoke to is not the woman who has been seeing me the past couple of weeks," I told him. "They have distinctly different voices and dress styles. This morning I heard the voice of a little girl."

"I think you just might be right about having a multiple personality on your hands," he said. "I seriously doubt Alice knows about Liz."

I agreed with him. "I think Alice suspects something isn't right, though. She mentioned losing track of time, sometimes hours."

"That's a good indication," he said. "It's not going to be an easy case, Kate, and there's no guarantee you'll be able to integrate the personalities. You know how these things work."

I nodded. "I can probably get Alice Smithers to agree to counseling," I said, "but Liz Jones will be a problem."

"Just leave Lizzy to me," he said, giving me a wink. "I'll play her like a tune."

I laughed. "I could never love you as much as you love yourself."

"I could teach you."

I arrived back at work and was surprised to find the hall door unlocked, as well as the door leading to my private office. Had I been in such a rush to get to the hospital that I'd forgotten to lock up?

I stepped inside, flipped the light switch, and gaped when I saw my file drawer standing open, a drawer I never forgot to lock. I felt a presence in the room even before I turned and saw him, before I heard the door close and the lock click into place.

He was in his thirties, not unattractive, but disheveled and unshaven. I met his gaze, saw the rage, felt a ripple of fear in my gut.

"Who are you, and what are you doing in my office?" I said, sounding cool and professional even as my heart skipped a few beats.

"So you're Dr. Holly," he said, taking a moment to look me over. "You don't look so tough."

I recognized the lisp immediately. I noted his clenched fists. "Why are you here?" I said. "The statue is gone from my front flower bed. Why can't you people just leave me alone?"

He frowned. "Lady, I don't know what the hell you're talking about."

He stepped closer. I was surprised to smell alcohol on him. "Who *are* you?" He didn't answer, but suddenly I knew. I also knew what he was capable of: I'd seen his handiwork.

"You turned Liz against me," Roy said. "You ruined everything."

"She came to me for help," I said. Which was only partially true, because Alice Smithers was the personality who'd sought me out.

"You messed with her head. I don't know what the hell you did to her, but she's all screwed up."

"If you leave now, I won't call the police." It was a lie, of course.

He drew back and slapped me so hard that I stumbled and fell to the floor. I tasted blood. I tried to stand, but he put his foot on me and held me down.

"She and I had big plans for that money. What did you say to her? What did you do that made her change her mind?"

"What money? I don't know anything about any money."

"The blackmail money!" he said between gritted teeth. He leaned over and slapped me again.

I cried out. He covered my mouth with one hand, grabbed my hair with the other, and yanked me to my feet. "I'll bet you convinced her to split it with you so you wouldn't go to the cops. I'll bet it's in this office. It didn't just disappear into thin air."

"I don't know what blackmail money you're talking about!"

"Stop lying!" he shouted. "You've got two seconds to tell me where it is!"

Frantically, I tried to put the pieces together. My mind raced; I grappled for answers. Who was Liz trying to blackmail? The only person who came to mind was the boss. Alice had mentioned an affair, but she did not strike me as a blackmailer. Liz, on the other hand, did.

"He was screwing her brains out," Roy said. "Then, when he got bored with her, he wanted to fire her. She deserved that money; *we* deserved it. It was the perfect plan until you came along."

It was too soon to know, and multiple personality

disorders could get confusing as hell, but I had obviously "botched" the plan by convincing Alice, possibly the host personality, to stand up for herself. She had stood up to Roy.

I struggled, but I was no match for his strength. Finally I bit his hand hard. He yanked it away, and I screamed.

"You're dead, lady."

I twisted in his arms and raked my nails down his face with my good hand. Every instinct in my body told me to fight, and the surprise on his face made it clear he hadn't expected it.

He grabbed my neck and squeezed. The look in his eyes told me he would not think twice about killing me. Mustering every bit of strength I had, I brought my knee up, found my target. He groaned; his eyes crossed; his grip loosened. I screamed again. He recovered quickly, and his hands felt stronger on my throat. I lost oxygen, began sinking to the floor, felt my knees hit the carpet. The gig was up.

Then the door to my office crashed open. A giant wearing a chest shield appeared suddenly. He leapt across the room, drawing an enormous sword. He put it to Roy's throat.

"Let her go or die," the giant said.

Roy's eyes registered fear and confusion, and he let me go. "Who the hell are you?" he asked.

"Omar the Great. Make one move, and I cut your

head off your shoulders and hang it from my rearview mirror."

A tidal wave of relief flooded me. Then it drew me under, and I sank into blackness.

"Katie, wake up!"

Somebody was shaking me. I struggled, started to scream again, and found Jay's face in front of me. I cried out and threw my arms around him. "Roy tried to kill me!" My voice was a rasp.

"You're safe now, babe," he said, putting his hand on my cheek.

I raised my head. Omar still had his sword at Roy's throat. I looked at Jay. "What are you doing here?" I asked. "Not that I'm complaining."

"I've been trying to call you," he said.

I remembered turning off my phone at the hospital. Obviously I'd forgotten to turn it back on.

"When I heard they couldn't find Roy, I got the sneaking suspicion he might show up here."

"You were right," I said. I looked at Omar. "Thank you." He bowed slightly.

Jay reached for his cell phone. "I'm calling it in," he said. "Do you need an ambulance?"

I shook my head. "My throat hurts, that's all."

"It's called attempted murder. Try to rest your voice, Katie."

* * *

By Friday I was feeling calmer. Roy was in jail. He had pled not guilty to attempted murder, but thanks to Omar, I had the proof I needed.

I arrived at the office at eight a.m., only to learn that my nine o'clock appointment had canceled. I wasn't annoyed. It would give me time to relax with a good cup of coffee.

For the fair, I'd chosen to wear my yellow daisy outfit. I had hoped the bright colors would energize me. I was still waiting for that to happen as I stood at the window overlooking the parking lot outside the office building. The scene resembled one of those carnivals that appear out of nowhere and set up in front of some strip mall.

I dreaded having to spend the afternoon shaking hands with people. I wanted to go home. I wanted to spend time with Mike and her puppies.

"My first appointment canceled," I told Mona when she arrived at eight thirty and met me in my office. I gazed out my window onto the parking lot, where a concession stand advertised hot dogs and cotton candy. "Oh, and I called my attorney. He's taking a deposition at the courthouse and can't be interrupted. Please let me know the minute he calls back."

"Are you calling off the divorce?" she asked.

"I'm going to see if it can be postponed. Jay and I should probably have a long talk." I watched a man lead a llama from a horse trailer. "Mona, why is there a llama in the parking lot?"

She joined me. "I had ordered a pony for the kids to ride, but his owner called a couple of days ago. The pony hurt one of his hooves and will be out of commission for a while."

I looked at her. "You know, I would never have thought of a llama."

She smiled brightly. "That's why I'm the publicist and you're not. Does Jay know you want to put the divorce on hold?"

"I haven't been able to reach him either."

Mona just looked at me.

"What?" I asked.

"You heard that old abandoned mill in Cabbagetown went up in flames sometime around midnight, right?"

"No!"

"I think they called in every fire department within a fifty-mile radius. I'm not surprised. That mill takes up an entire city block."

"Well, I'm not going to freak out over it," I said. "That building is scheduled for demolition. There's a big *X* over the door, and it's boarded up big-time. Firefighters would not perform a search and rescue, and they'd fight it from the outside."

"What if somebody had managed to get in?" Mona asked. "What if it was rumored to have a couple of homeless people sleeping there?"

I tensed. "That would change everything."

"I'm just repeating what I heard on the news downstairs in the coffee shop," she almost whispered.

Five minutes later Mona and I, along with several other customers, were glued to the TV set in Hot Spot coffee and pastry shop on the first floor.

The fire had been extinguished, but there were still a number of firefighters on the scene. The camera closed in on their faces, lines of exhaustion embedded with ash. In the background stood a charred brick building gutted by fire.

I knew Jay had been among the men who'd battled the blaze. I knew that Jay would not hesitate to go into a burning building if there was a chance someone was inside. He had the commendations to prove it. Jay was not a captain who sat behind a desk. He was hands-on. He gave the orders, and he went inside if he thought his men needed him.

I tried his cell once more. No answer.

I stared at the TV. The newsman was trying to find out the number of men injured or sent to the hospital with smoke inhalation. No deaths reported as yet. I closed my eyes. Multiplication tables fired through my brain, riding on waves of adrenaline. "I hate this," I told Mona.

"Why don't you go back upstairs, and I'll let you know the second I hear anything."

I started to argue.

"You can't do anything, Kate," she said. "Besides, you're waiting to hear from your attorney."

I'd forgotten. And Mona was right. There was nothing I could do except wait.

I left the coffee shop and caught the elevator to the fourth floor. I stepped inside my office and was startled to find George Moss pacing the reception room, holding his vial. And here I thought the day couldn't get worse.

"What are you doing here?" I demanded. "I told you I would not be treating you in the future."

"You had no right to dismiss me. You and your receptionist probably find me laughable. A foolish old man," he added. "Well, your first mistake was not taking me seriously." He shoved the vial in my face.

My temper flared. Enough was enough, dammit! "You know what, George? I've had a crummy couple of days. You want to blow me up? Well, go right ahead. Make my day!"

He looked surprised, uncertain.

I snatched the vial from his hand.

George's eyes shot open wide. "Don't drop that!"

"Why not, George?" I ignored him and began to toss it in the air with my good hand. He ducked and put his hands over his head.

"You're crazy!" he yelled.

"People like you *make* me crazy! You want to blow up my office? Here, let me do it for you!"

George screamed as I threw the vial as hard as I could against the opposite wall. He pushed me to the floor a split second before the explosion that shattered the window and sent glass flying in all directions.

I screamed.

Four hours later, dressed in jeans and a baggy T-shirt, I pulled my car beside a park and, snapping Mike's leash to her collar, helped her from the front seat. I'd been driving for an hour, just driving around in no particular direction, and now I figured Mike needed to find a bush.

I was still sore after being shoved to the floor by George. I was covered with cuts and scratches; Bobo the Knife had picked shards of glass from those body parts that had been exposed during the explosion. George Moss had been treated and taken away in handcuffs. It was hard to feel sympathy for the man. He had ruined my favorite outfit.

I was numb now, but it beat the hell out of stark terror, which is precisely what I'd felt upon hearing the explosion and watching my window be blown to smithereens. Even worse was having George heave himself on top of me, his bony, liver-spotted chest in my face. I thought of the nightmares that awaited me about that chest.

I'd refused to let Mona call anyone, and for once she had not argued with me. I think she knew I was one step away from going completely over the edge. I'd lain on the bed in the exam room until my knees had stopped trembling, and I'd watched the minutes tick by on the large wall clock. I had not bothered to call my attorney again. I'd watched eleven a.m. come and go, marking my divorce.

I found an empty park bench and sat down. As though she sensed that I needed comforting, Mike hopped on the bench beside me and snuggled close. She licked the scratches on my hand. And when she rose on her hind legs and licked the single tear on my cheek, I knew there was a reason we had found each other when we did. I had already decided to keep her, and I would see that her puppies were placed in good homes.

I stroked her gently, leaned my head back, and closed my eyes. The sun felt good on my face. I tried to imagine it seeping into my pores, healing me.

Jay and I had spent a lot of time at the park early in our marriage; it brought back bittersweet memories of picnics and the sound of children's laughter.

I dozed, only to jerk awake when I realized someone was standing before me. I opened my eyes and found Jay staring down at me, his face gray and lined with worry and exhaustion. He wore a business suit.

"Dammit, Kate!" he all but shouted. "I have been looking all over this town for you. I heard about the explosion after I got out of court." He muttered a couple more four-letter words and sank onto the bench.

I wanted to reach out to him, but his anger was palpable. I waited.

"Just so you know, it scared the holy hell out of me," he said.

"It scared the llama too."

He gave me an odd look. "Are you okay, Katie? I mean, are you *really* okay?" His blue eyes scanned me from head to toe. I saw the pained look in his eyes as he took in the cuts and bruises. "Bobo assured me you'd be fine, but I had to see for myself. I waited on your front steps for close to an hour. I thought I'd go crazy."

"I'm okay, Jay. Are you okay?"

"Yeah, I'm good."

He very gently enfolded me in his arms, and we sat quietly, holding on tight to each other. I inhaled his scent, felt him tremble. He pulled back slightly and looked at me.

"Katie, I would never try to tell you what to do, but your job is dangerous. There are some really sick people out there, and I think you're the one treating all of them."

I chuckled. "Fortunately most of them are behind bars now." He pulled me close once more, taking care with my injuries.

"How was our divorce?" I asked.

He sighed. "Quick. People shouldn't be able to get divorced so easily. They should have to try harder. *We* should have tried harder."

I'd been trying to hold back my tears, but I could no longer contain them. They came hard and fast. They came from way down deep and spilled over. Mike climbed into my lap, and Jay continued to hold me.

"Go ahead and let it out, Katie," he said gently. "You earned it."

Finally the tears stopped. I was exhausted, but the hurt was not as raw.

"Listen to me, Katie," Jay said in a voice so tender that it was hard to believe he was the same man who had fought a ravenous fire only hours before. "I'm not going to put any more pressure on you than you're already dealing with," he said. "We don't have to make any important decisions about us right now. I just want you to be okay, and I want you to be happy. Whatever it takes," he added.

"Waffles would be nice," I said. "And then a nap."

He chuckled and pressed his lips to my forehead. "You got it, babe. Your place or mine?"

My name is Kate Holly. As a clinical psychologist, I get paid to listen to other people's problems. You wouldn't believe some of the stuff I hear. And just when I think I've heard it all, a new patient will come in and prove me wrong.

I'm here to tell you that the whole world is nuts. Even worse, I sometimes worry that I'm more screwed up than most of my patients. For one thing, I'm obsessive-compulsive. When I'm stressed I count things. I do multiplication tables in my head. I prefer even numbers because they are divisible by two. Odd numbers are complicated.

Sort of like my life.

Most of my colleagues jokingly agree that it's hard to tell the doctors from the patients and we should all be fitted for straitjackets.

At least some of my neuroses come from my mother and my aunt. I know they aren't normal, but damned if I can find an accurate diagnosis for them in the *DSM*, otherwise known as the *Diagnostic and Statistical Manual of Mental Disorders*. I think that's scary.

Even before my father, a fireman, died in the line of duty when I was ten, my mother and my aunt were hardcore junk dealers. I was forced to get up at dawn and pick through the trash in ritzy neighborhoods on garbage day while they kept watch from their battered pickup truck, the engine running so we could make a quick getaway if we had to. I was coaxed inside every Dumpster within a fifty mile radius, and I knew everybody's name at the local flea market where we rented a booth on weekends.

Naturally, the kids at school found out about the family junk business. It was hard to miss since our house looked like something out of *Sanford & Son*. Which was how my mother and aunt became known as the Junk Sisters, and I became the laughingstock.

Even worse, my mother and my aunt are identical twins who still dress alike. Picture two plus-sized women in their mid-fifties with big platinum hair and inch-long eyelashes, wearing red overalls with the words *Junk Sisters* stitched over their left breasts. Red is their signature color, which explains why their six-ton 2007 Navistar CLT is candy apple red. It's twenty-one feet long and hauls a lot of junk. They've furnished my office and my rental house with junk. I allow it because I can't afford to buy decent furniture, and because I don't want to hurt their feelings.

Sometimes, when I'm at the end of my rope with these women, I can't help but wonder if my father chose to stay in that burning building on purpose.

I guess you could say I have issues.

I also have issues with my now ex-husband. I must've been making decisions out of my behind when I agreed to marry him because, guess what, he's a firefighter just like my father. I pretty much white-knuckled my way through three years of marriage before a building collapsed on him and his crew, sending them to the ER in an ambulance. Once I discovered their injuries weren't life-threatening, I packed my bags. I thought if given a choice between me and his career, my husband would have chosen me hands down. I waited four months for him to beg me to come home before I gave up and filed for a divorce. It was sort of a face-saving thing.

Then, two weeks before our divorce became final, we ended up in bed. It wasn't my fault. I was drinking champagne on an empty stomach at the time.

The long and the short of it was, after two months of so-called dating, we'd decided to try and save our relationship.

Which explained why we were sitting in a marriage counselor's office.

Evelyn Hunt came highly recommended even though she's the highest priced couples therapist in Atlanta. It's obvious her clients paid their bills regularly, unlike most of mine, because Evelyn's office looked like the showroom floor at Ethan Allen. She wasted no time getting down to business.

"How's the sex?" she asked.

The question startled me. I had done my share of marriage counseling, and I had posed that very same question to troubled couples. But this was the first time someone had asked me.

I glanced at Jay. He smiled. I smiled. "It's great," I said. Evelyn looked at Jay.

"It's pretty good," he said, nodding.

My smile faded slightly. "Pretty good?" I blurted, wondering if he was just trying to be funny. Or maybe the question had caught him off guard as well.

He shifted in his chair. The blue nylon jacket he wore matched his eyes. He'd shoved the sleeves to his elbows, exposing arms that were brown and corded with muscle. He worked hard to stay in shape, and it showed. That, combined with his thick dark hair and olive complexion, had turned more heads than mine. And I'm here to tell you, I almost wet my pants the first time I saw him naked.

"Sometimes I wonder if you're using sex so we don't have to talk about our problems," he said.

My mouth flew open. "That's not true!" Okay, maybe it *was* true, I admitted to myself. But after listening to other people's problems all day, the last thing I wanted to do when I closed shop was talk about ours.

"Sometimes I feel—" Jay paused. "—like you're holding back," he said. "Like part of you is cut off from me."

Oh, jeez. When had the man gone all touchy-feely on me? "How can you say that?"

"I could have it all wrong, Katie, but that's how I feel."

Evelyn turned from Jay to me. "Do you think you hold back?" she asked.

"I'm open to him," I said, feeling the need to defend myself in front of Evelyn now that she thought I was a nymphomaniac. "I share." But I knew it wasn't the whole truth and nothing but the truth. I hadn't told Jay I was being evicted from my office over an incident that happened two months ago. I was convinced I could change my landlord's mind. I'd failed, and now I had less than a week to get out.

"Have you tried to discuss your feelings with Kate?" Evelyn asked Jay.

He shrugged. "I've wanted to, but we always end up in bed."

I sank lower in my chair. I could feel Evelyn's eyes on me. Jay and I *had* spent much of the past eight weeks since our divorce naked. It was the reason we made reservations at our favorite restaurants and never showed, the reason we'd missed two films we'd wanted to see, and lost money on concert tickets Jay had purchased.

"You should have told me how you felt," I said.

His gaze softened. "I figured you'd been through enough." He looked at Evelyn. "First, one of her patients almost ran over her in his car, and she ended up in the ER with a fractured wrist—"

"My patient did *not* try to run over me," I told Evelyn. "I was chasing him across the parking lot and I tripped. My patient went out of his way to keep from hitting me with his car."

"Then, the boyfriend of another patient tries to kill her," he went on.

"Oh, my!" Evelyn said.

I opened my mouth to protest but Jay cut me off. "Kate survived that, only to have another patient show up with nitroglycerin, and—" He sighed and ran one hand down his face. "She blew up her office."

Evelyn gaped at me. "You blew up your office!"

"He's exaggerating. I only blew out a window in my office." I sat up straighter. "There's a perfectly reasonable explanation," I added.

"You could have died!" Jay said.

"So now you know how *I* feel!" I said. I turned to Evelyn. "I become paralyzed with fear every time he's called to a fire. My father was a fireman and died in the line of duty," I added.

Jay and I argued back and forth for a few minutes. Finally, Evelyn looked at her watch. "Our time is up for the day." She sounded relieved. "I'd like to give you both some homework in the meantime."

She looked at Jay. "I want you to try to be as patient and understanding toward Kate as you can be while she works through her fears." Jay nodded and she turned to me. "I'd like to see you open up more to Jay instead of using sex as a diversion."

My face burned. I opened my mouth to protest, then closed it and nodded.

Jay walked me to my car. It was the last week of October, and, after a summer of soaring heat that threatened to fry your lungs each time you took a breath, the nippy air was a welcome relief.

"Are you okay?" Jay asked.

"We suck at marriage."

"We don't suck at marriage." He put his arms around me and kissed the top of my head. "We're just trying to work out the kinks. It'll be okay, Katie."

I leaned into the hug, hoping that some of his optimism would rub off on me. His body was strong and solid; I could feel his heat seeping through my clothes. "I know," I finally said. But I *didn't* know, and that's what worried me.

I heard loud singing before I opened the door to my reception room. Inside, I found a fortysomething woman standing on a chair and belting out the words to "Over the Rainbow." That she sang off-key did not seem to concern her. The fact that I wasn't *surprised* to find a complete stranger performing a nightclub act in my office says a lot about what I face on a daily basis.

My receptionist, Mona Epps, gave me an eye roll.

I simply stood there quietly while the woman sang, using a hairbrush as her microphone. Finally, she finished. I smiled and clapped and Mona did likewise.

"Who are you?" the woman asked, stepping down from the chair.

"I'm Dr. Kate Holly," I said. "You can call me Kate." I smiled. "And you are?"

"Marie Osmond. Most people don't recognize me at first. They say I look younger in person."

"Don't feel bad," Mona said to me. "I didn't recognize her either."

"How can I help you?" I asked the woman, even though my first thought was to suggest voice lessons.

She stepped closer. "I'm in a lot of danger. One of my fans is stalking me."

"Did you report it to the police?" Dumb question to ask a delusional person, I thought.

"They didn't believe me. I've been hiding for days. Then I saw your phone number written in the sky, with the words, 'Your Compassionate Friend,' and I knew right away it was a sign from God."

I gave an inward sigh. The minute somebody tells me they've received a sign from God I know I'm either dealing with a psychotic or a Jehovah's Witness. It was hard to be sure in this case, however, since Mona has been paying a pilot to pull a banner through the skies of Atlanta advertising my services. Mona, who appointed herself as my publicist, is determined to catapult me to fame so that I can have my own TV or radio talk show. Since Mona is rich and spends her own money, there's not much I can do about it.

"You've come to the right place," I told the woman. "Is there someone I can call? A close friend or relative? Your doctor?" I added hopefully. I had a feeling the woman belonged in the psych ward, and it would be less complicated if her next of kin could commit her. Not only did I lack a patient history on her, she wasn't carrying a purse, which meant she had no ID on her. Only a hairbrush.

She shook her head. "There is no one."

"What about Donny?" Mona asked.

I looked at Mona. She shrugged.

"Donny and I don't sing together anymore," she said. She sighed. "Families can be such a pain in the ass."

I nodded. It was the first sane thing that had come out of her mouth.

"I'm tired now," the Marie Osmond wannabe said, "and I have a second show to perform this evening. I haven't slept much lately. I've been on the run from the sicko who is after me."

"You *look* exhausted," I told her. "You should take some time off and rest."

"You mean cancel my tour? I can't just take off on some silly vacation and ignore my fans!"

I knew I was in trouble. If she had a problem going on vacation she wasn't going to be receptive to hospitalization. Sometimes, though, it's the only way, especially when there is no family to help out. "Don't you think your safety is more important?" I asked. She seemed to consider it.

"Why don't we go into my office and discuss your options." I opened the door and motioned her through, then I turned to Mona. "Would you please get Thad on the phone?"

"Uh-oh," Mona said. She flipped through the Rolodex on her desk. "He's going to expect something in return. Especially now that you're officially divorced," she added.

Dr. Thad Glazer was my ex-boyfriend, and the center of his universe. He was also a psychiatrist to the wealthy, meaning he never worried about his patients' checks bouncing. I'd broken it off with Thad four years ago when I caught him cheating. I'd later met and married Jay. Thad still believes I did it to get back at him. Now that I was divorced, he thought we should pick up where we'd left off. Despite it all, I could pretty much count on him to see my patients for medication therapy; in return, I took on his more troublesome patients for talk therapy.

"I'll be right back," I said. I stepped inside my office and found Marie lying on my sofa. I went through a mental checklist of what she might actually be suffering from.

I covered her with a light throw and returned to the reception room.

Mona held up the phone. "Thad's on the line."

I grabbed it. "I've got a delusional woman in my office," I told him. "I'm going to have to admit her to the hospital. She's going to need meds."

Thad chuckled. "That sort of places you in the predicament of needing me," he said.

"Yeah, okay." It was easier to play along.

He gave a wistful sigh. "Say the words, Kate."

"I need you, Thad." Mona shook her head sadly.

"I'll have to reschedule my tennis match," he said. "I wish you had called me yesterday when I had more time on my hands."

"I'm sorry you'll be forced to spend the afternoon actually practicing psychiatry instead of your backhand," I said, trying to sound sympathetic.

"You're not sorry. Which brings me to the next question," he said. "What's in it for me?"

I'd been subconsciously waiting for Thad to say something inappropriate, because that's what he did. He pushed my buttons, yanked my chain, and all of the above. As a thirty-two-year-old professional, I knew I should try to rise above it. I seldom did.

"Do you know how immature you sound?" I said. "Besides, you owe me. Does the name George Moss ring a bell?"

"Are you going to hold that against me forever?" Thad asked. "How was I supposed to know he was *really* carrying nitroglycerin in his insulin vial?"

"It would have been nice to ask someone at a lab to check it out before sending him to *me*. I could have been killed."

"Well, he's not going to bother you anymore so I was hoping we could put it behind us and start fresh. We need to talk about us."

"There is no 'us,' Thad."

"Kate, Kate, Kate. I know you've been through a rough time, but you have to move on. I could help you forget Jay Rush ever existed."

I knew Thad's remedy for everything from stress to ingrown toenails was a pitcher of margaritas and a stint in his hot tub, followed by all-night sex. The only thing likely to make me forget Jay was a full frontal lobotomy.

"I have to go, Thad," I said. "I'll see you later at the hospital."

He acquiesced with a sigh. I hung up and handed the phone to Mona.

"Was he trying to talk you into having phone sex?" she asked.

"Not this time."

"So am I supposed to call and see if there is room at the loony bin?"

I had corrected Mona many times when she made fun of my patients, but she did it anyway. I let it slide because she was my best friend and answered my phone for free, a huge plus for me since I was trying to build my practice.

"Go ahead and call the hospital," I said. "I'm going to see if I can get any more information out of Miss Osmond."

I was waiting for an ambulance to pick up the woman napping in my office when my next patient, Eddie Franks, arrived. Eddie had spent a number of years in prison for conning several old ladies out of their retirement. Weekly therapy sessions were one of the conditions of his parole. In his late fifties, Eddie was handsome, impeccably dressed, and the smoothest-talking man I'd ever met. Except for my ex-husband, who could talk your panties off before you had time to remove your coat.

I motioned for Eddie to follow me down the hall to my small kitchenette. "I have an emergency this morning," I said. "We're not going to be able to work in a full session today."

"Just as long as you tell my parole officer I was here," Eddie said, smiling. His teeth were too perfect to be his own. He hid his bald spot with a comb-over technique and a lot of hairspray.

"How was your week?" I asked quickly.

"I found a job," he announced proudly. "I'm working for a very prestigious menswear store. I'm their newest salesman."

"Congratulations," I said. "It's the perfect job for you since you're so particular about your clothes."

"I plan to work my way up to manager. Who knows, maybe I'll have my own store one day."

"Slow down, Eddie," I said, although it was easy to get caught up in his enthusiasm. "You need to take it one day at a time and follow through with the conditions of your parole." I did not want Eddie to backslide into his old habits.

"I can't help being impatient," he said. "I wasted a lot of time behind bars."

I nodded. I liked Eddie, but it bothered me that he was more focused on how his crimes had affected *him*. He spent very little time thinking about the women he'd cheated. I wanted to hear remorse. I wanted Eddie to be sorry for what he'd done and not just give me lip service.

"Knock, knock," Mona said, standing in the doorway. "Your mom and your aunt just showed up. They decided to surprise you and take you to lunch."

"Aren't I booked for the day?" I asked hopefully.

"Yep. That's what I told them. Oh, and the ambulance will be here in a few minutes," she said.

I looked at Eddie. "I have to run. We can set up another time this week if you like."

"Don't worry about me, Dr. Holly," he said. "I'll be fine. I'm a changed man."

I hurried toward the reception area, where I found my mother and aunt thumbing through magazines. It would have been hard to miss them. "Good morning," I said.

My mother looked at me. "You're too thin." She turned to my aunt. "Doesn't Kate look thin?"

"I think she looks great," my aunt said.

My aunt was the family peacemaker and spent much of her time trying to smooth out the misunderstandings between my mother and me.

My mother looked annoyed. "Trixie, how can you say Kate looks good when she's practically skin and bones?" She turned to me. "Are you sick? You can tell me, you know."

I debated telling her that I had mad cow disease. "I'm fine," I said instead. I couldn't really blame her for being concerned about my weight, though. My separation and divorce had whittled me from a size ten to a six. Mona's housekeeper, Mrs. Perez, had taken in a lot of my clothes since I couldn't afford to buy a new wardrobe.

"We came by to see if you could have lunch with us," Aunt Trixie said, changing the subject.

My mother nodded. "You'll have to hurry on account of we're double-parked."

I envisioned their monster pickup truck piled high with junk, blocking half the cars in the parking lot. "I'm sorry, but I can't go," I said. I noted Eddie Franks eyeing them curiously, but I wasn't surprised. "I have an emergency."

"Are you hurt?" my mother asked, one hand flying to her breast as she carefully studied me from head to toe.

"It's one of my patients," I said quickly.

Eddie stepped forward. "Dr. Holly, I insist that you introduce me to these gorgeous women."

I looked at him. The man could really turn on the charm. Which was why I wasn't crazy about the idea of introducing him to my mother and my aunt. Unfortunately, I couldn't think of a way to get out of it without appearing rude.

"Mr. Franks, I'd like for you to meet my mother and my aunt, Dixie and Trixie." I decided not to give him their last names so he wouldn't be able to look them up in the phone book.

"Eddie Franks," he said, making a production of taking each of their hands and pressing his lips to them. "I can see where Dr. Holly gets her beauty."

Both women fluttered their inch-long lashes at him, stirring up more air than my ceiling fan.

The door to my office opened, and the woman whose real name I still did not know stepped out. Her clothes were wrinkled and her hair mussed from her brief nap. "I can't sleep with all this noise," she asked. "How am I supposed to perform tonight?"

Everyone looked at her. "I'm sorry," I said. "Your ride will be here any minute. You'll be able to get all the rest you need."

"You're a performer?" my aunt asked.

The woman looked insulted. "You don't recognize me? It just so happens I'm Marie Osmond."

My mother shot me a look of annoyance. "*Now* I know

why you're being so secretive. You could have just said you had a famous person in your office that you didn't want us to see."

Aunt Trixie stepped forward, reached for the woman's hand and began pumping it enthusiastically. "Oh, I'm a *huge* fan," she said. "I still have all your Christmas tapes." She paused. "You look different in person."

"Well, to be perfectly honest, I'm in disguise so I'm not all that surprised you didn't recognize me. Would you like for me to sing something for you?"

Without warning, the woman began singing "Over the Rainbow" again.

The door to the reception room opened, and a patient, Arnie Decker, walked through. He stopped short, as though he didn't know what to make of the crowd gathered in my reception room or the woman singing at the top of her voice.

Eddie did a double take at the sight of Arnie, a retired Marine who claimed he was trapped in a woman's body. Despite his broad shoulders, and a large tattoo of an eagle on one bulging bicep, he was dressed in short shorts and a glittery high-rise T-shirt that exposed his pierced navel. That was lame compared to his polished toenails, all ten of them peeking out the tops of his beaded sandals.

"Hello, Mr. Decker," I said. "You can wait for me in my office." He nodded and went inside.

My mother looked at me. "I don't know how you deal with this sort of thing day after day," she said. "I'd go crazy. No wonder you're depressed. No wonder you're so thin."

"I'm not depressed, Mom," I said, trying to make myself heard above the singing.

She looked at Trixie. "I told you we were wasting our time coming here. I told you Kate would be too busy for us."

"Ladies!" Eddie said. "Please allow me to take you to lunch."

I felt my jaw drop open.

They looked from him to me and back to him. "We don't even know you," my mother said.

"What better way to get acquainted than over lunch," he said. "It'll be my treat."

"Don't you have to get back to work?" I asked Eddie hopefully.

He shook his head. "I have plenty of time."

I didn't like it one bit. Eddie was known to work fast. It wouldn't take long for him to convince two unsuspecting women into investing their IRA account on a get-rich scheme that would end up filling Eddie's pockets.

"I don't think that's a good idea," I blurted, even though my hands were tied. It would have been unethical for me to pull my mother and my aunt aside and tell them about Eddie's shady past.

"Don't be silly," Eddie said. "I will take excellent care of your beautiful mother and aunt." He flashed a movie star smile.

"I suppose it'll be okay," my mother said. My aunt nodded in agreement.

The discussion was interrupted when the door to the reception room opened once again. Two paramedics stepped inside. I recognized one of the men. Carter was an old friend of Jay's who had attended a couple of Christmas parties at our loft before I'd moved out.

"Hi, Kate," he said, trying to make himself heard over the woman's booming voice. "We're here to pick up Marie Osmond."

"We should skedaddle," Eddie said, "and let Dr. Holly do her job." He ushered my mother and aunt out before I could stop them.

Finally, the woman stopped singing. "I hope you're taking me to a safe place," she said. "I've got this nutso fan stalking me."

Carter offered his arm. "I guarantee you'll be perfectly safe," he assured her. "If you'll allow us to escort you, we'll be on our way."

"I'll be in touch," I told him as Mona and I watched them lead the woman out.

I sighed and sank into a chair.

"What's wrong?" Mona said. "I think it went pretty well."

"Hello?" I waved my hand at her. "Eddie Franks, the great bamboozler of women, just took my mother and aunt to lunch." I didn't discuss my patient's diagnoses with Mona because it would have been unethical. But Eddie, just like most of those who sought my counsel, told Mona everything before I ever spoke with them. Mona thought nothing of offering them advice.

She suddenly smacked her forehand with one hand. "Uh-oh." She took the chair next to me. "Guess you know what that means."

I looked at her.

"You can kiss off your inheritance."